N
0 25 50 100
Scale of Miles
DISTRICT
Kopa's and Zack Denny's route through the LOST LANDS of Mackenzie District in NORTHWEST CANADA
GREAT BEAR LAKE
ARCTIC CIRCLE

OX

Sam dearest —
from Mum + Dad with
Xmas 1944 — love + joy + pride

NORTHERN TRAIL ADVENTURE

BOOKS BY WEST LATHROP

JUNEAU: THE SLEIGH DOG

MONKEY AHOY!

NORTHERN TRAIL ADVENTURE

West Lathrop

RANDOM HOUSE · New York

To my nephews

Thomas, Miles and Daniel

Published simultaneously in Canada by Random House of Canada Ltd.

PRINTED IN THE UNITED STATES OF AMERICA

CONTENTS

CHAPTER ONE

Zachariah Denny Meets a Stranger

THE small log cabin by the dwarf spruce was a welcome sight to Zack Denny's tired eyes. In a final burst of speed, the dogs drew the sled halfway up the gully right of the cabin and stopped. With one accord they turned their heads and looked back at him, remembering that they had left the sled there a few months before.

"Good dogs," said the man.

The poor beasts were as tired as he was. Unharnessed and staked, they lost no time in gulping down their dried fish and curling up in the lee of a snow drift. All but Moise, the big white leader, who broke loose and disappeared in the direction of the cabin. Zack dragged the sled farther up the gully to a spot where the snow was shallow and then knelt to untie the lashings which held his pack. In a few moments, there would be a fire in the small stove in the cabin. After some hot tea he would crawl into his bag. Sleep! He was in desperate need of sleep!

The pack loosened, Zack stood up and looked to the west. Clouds were banked, heavy and gray, where only an hour before the sky had been clear. The storm would break at any moment. Except for patches of scrub growth which grew along the frozen river to the north, a bleak white world lay before him. Nothing stirred . . .

The wind which had been pushing at his back for the last hour had suddenly ceased. There were no longer the bump and scrape of the sled runners, the jangle of the sled bell, the scratch of the dogs' feet on the ice . . . sounds which had beat in his ears all that day. But in a few moments a frenzy of wind would sweep in from the west, crying in a thousand voices, tearing at the small log cabin and the single tree. How well he had come to know the ominous silence which preceded every storm!

Zack stooped, shouldered his pack and swung the dogs' harnesses over his arm, just as Moise came tearing around the corner of the cabin. Moise was crying in short high yelps as he followed a trail.

"Hare," said Zack to himself, marveling at Moise's endurance. The other dogs were already asleep, round fur balls with bushy tails over their noses.

"What's the matter?" asked Zack as he drew nearer. Then he stopped abruptly in his tracks.

A thin wisp of smoke curled upward from the tin chimney against the grey sky. Somebody had just left the cabin! But there had been no recent tracks on the trail which he had just come over. No doubt a party had come in from the west and returned the same way. However, to leave a shelter now was foolhardy. Only an errand of life or death would force anyone to march into the coming blizzard. The next cabin was miles away!

Zack scanned the snow for footprints. There they

were, the round-toed imprints of snowshoes entering the cabin. But there were no signs of snowshoes coming out of the cabin and Zack paused, perplexed. He decided that as soon as he had dropped his pack inside, he would go down the trail a bit to see where the stranger had left his sled and dogs. Moise was now scratching frantically at the corner of the door.

"Back, Moise, back! G'wan, mush!" The dog drew back as Zack kicked at the door which opened on creaking hinges. "Halloa, there!" he called.

There was no answer, so he entered, careful to close the door quickly to conserve the cabin's heat. Dropping his pack, he gazed about him.

A pan of water with tea dregs still left at the bottom was on the stove. A parka with wolverine-trimmed hood hung back of the door, and snowshoes, apparently discarded in haste, lay on the floor. There was no doubt that the cabin was occupied! Leaning forward, Zack peered about. Upon a rough plank bed lay a figure curled in a sleeping bag.

"Tuckered out," said Zack to himself. "Well, so'm I. But what's he doing here without a sled?" Crossing the room to a small pile of wood in a corner, he stood and surveyed it. "Half gone," he grumbled. "He's been here a day anyway. Halloa!" he called again. Moise whined at the door but there was no other sound.

A kettle of water stood at the back of the stove. Zack added wood to the fire, pulled the kettle forward, and while he waited for the water to boil, glanced at the parka on the back of the door.

"It's well made," he observed. "Eskimo sewing."

Some knee boots of sealskin lay beneath the plank bed, and these caught his eye.

"Eskimo again," said Zack to himself.

The tea was hot and black. Using a wooden box for a seat, Zack drank three cups. But his hands were shaking with fatigue and his eyes stinging as he bent forward to take off his deerskin boots. As he slid into his bag on the floor, he was half conscious that the storm had come. Flakes, hard and dry and fine, beat against the single window with the sound of sifting sand, and the wind swept past the cabin with a scream.

"Just in time," murmured the man. "Just in time," he repeated dully and slid deeper into his bag. And almost instantly, he was asleep.

Five years of life on northern trails had hardened Zack Denny to many unusual sights. He had quartered with Eskimos in their ice houses and with Indians in their tepees. He had shared many a roof and simple meal with sourdoughs and adventurers from Outside, but he was not prepared for the sight which greeted him when he opened his eyes that next morning. As his head came out of the warm depths of his bag, he was conscious of the crackle of burning wood. A pale grey light filtering through the window revealed the slight figure of a person dressed in deerskin pants and green flannel shirt bending over the wood pile. Zack stirred. The figure straightened instantly and turned around.

"Halloa," said Zack.

A boy nodded his head. Beneath the brown wool cap with fur ear laps were dark eyes which gazed at him with a cautious and wary expression. Giving no other sign of recognition, the boy crossed the room, his moccasined feet making no sound, and put a stick of wood on the fire. Zack looked after him and then slowly unzipped his bag. Perhaps, he reasoned, the stranger could not speak English. Nevertheless, as he pulled on his boots he decided to try again.

"Where you from?" he asked distinctly and slowly.

There was a short silence. Then, "Coldhill," answered the boy.

"Coldhill! That's a long trek from here." Zack stared frankly at the stranger. He still wondered if the boy could speak English. "What'd you do . . . walk?" he asked, pointing at the snowshoes by the door.

"No."

The boy could talk, all right. He was now slicing bacon from the end of a slab with a short, sharp knife. The hand was not too steady and the slices were cut in a jagged manner.

"My name is Zachariah Denny. What's yours?"

Again that slight hesitation.

"Kop-a."

"Copper! C-o-p-p-e-r? I used to know someone named Copper over Wild River way . . ."

"I spell mine K-o-p-a."

"Kop-a," repeated Zack.

It sounded Eskimo. But this boy was no Eskimo. He was a white boy through and through. A white boy with an Eskimo name! And it was beginning to be evident that Kop-a did not wish to talk, nor did he welcome company. His indifference and independence would have been amusing but for the racking cough which seized him and shook him from head to foot. Zack waited until the coughing ceased and the boy had cooked his bacon and made tea. He was still perplexed. It took a hardened sourdough to keep alive in this wilderness east of the Mackenzie, north of Good Hope. And only men of experience traveled alone. Zack searched in his kit and pulled out a can of beans.

"I didn't stop along the trail for much food to-day. Was trying to beat the storm. Maybe you'll have some beans with me," he added cordially. "Guess we're in for it," and he squinted up at the window, "so we might as well be comfortable."

The dark eyes regarded him for an instant and then looked at the can of beans. Zack wondered if he saw a suppressed flicker of interest in their depths. Evidently not, for Kop-a shook his head. "Thanks," he said briefly, "I've had enough."

Zack warmed his beans and drank tea while the boy washed his tins and packed them in his kit. In the dim light, the young face appeared white and strained. There were hollows under the cheek bones and the mouth was set in a stubborn line.

An hour passed by. . . . Curled up in a corner, on top of his sleeping bag, Kop-a watched every move that Zack made. He seemed to be a person accustomed to long hours of silence with only his own thoughts for company. Once when he raised an arm and pushed back his wool cap, Zack's keen eyes noted that the hand was long and shapely but much too thin. The bones of the knuckles stood out sharply. Zack had seen thin hands before and knew the cause. The boy was underfed.

The morning passed slowly. Zack alternately tended the fire and dozed with his feet towards the stove, his back against the plank bed. Kop-a remained in the corner, half asleep, his eyes opening when Zack moved. Outside the storm continued to beat against the cabin with relentless fury. The window was now completely banked with snow and only the fire, showing between the wide cracks of the stove, served to lighten the room.

If the boy wished to be let alone, he was having his wish, Zack thought to himself. Several times the silence was broken by the hollow-sounding cough and finally pity softened the man. After one particularly hard spasm, he reached into his pack and brought out some sweet chocolate.

"Here," said Zack, "try some of that."

"Thanks," replied Kop-a, but he made no effort to pick it up.

Zack's wrist watch ticked into the late afternoon hours. Kop-a again cooked a few slices of bacon and drank more tea. Zack ate the rest of his beans and fried a small piece of caribou steak. If the meat smelled appetizing to the boy, he gave no sign.

"He's a gritty little devil," observed the man watching him closely. "I wonder how long he'll hold out."

For his own amusement, for he had now ceased to consider Kop-a's likes or dislikes, Zack dug to the depths of his pack and brought out a black leather case and some round black disks, the latter in flannel cases. He wound a handle, pressed a lever, and strains of music filled the small cabin, rising sweet and clear above the howl of the storm outside.

The boy sat upright. It was too dark to see his face but Zack heard him draw in his breath sharply. When the record was half finished, the man was suddenly aware that Kop-a stood beside him, his dark eyes staring at the small victrola. With the playing of the last note, the boy turned on his heel and went back to his corner.

To Zack's great relief, the wind shifted in the night, and morning brought a clearing of the storm. Although the snow was soft, he planned to continue on his journey. By breaking the trail ahead on snowshoes, he could make it easy for the dogs. It would be a help if Kop-a stayed on the sled and steered for him, but he had no idea what the boy wished to do and, moreover, he disliked to ask. A wall of silence had sprung up between them. However, Zack knew that if he left Kop-a there alone, it might trouble his conscience in the days to come. It would be another fortnight before Jon Mitchen came through with the mail and he knew that the boy's supplies were low. He decided to make one more decent gesture by offering to take the stranger as far as Henry's roadhouse. From then on, someone else could worry over him.

"I'm harnessing my dogs soon," he announced, "and then I'm hitting the trail again. Can I give you a lift?"

"A lift?" questioned the boy, looking directly at him with surprise in his voice. "You mean, don't you, that you're taking me to Henry's whether I want to go or not. You're not fooling me."

"What do you mean by that?" asked Zack, now aroused. "You can stay here and freeze to death if you wish to. It means nothing to me. What's the matter with you anyway? You haven't the courtesy or manners of the most ordinary trapper along the trail."

"I'm sorry." Kop-a's expression had changed swiftly and completely. The dark eyes had a pleading look in them and his mouth lost its stubborn set line. "It's my . . . it's my mistake, I guess. I thought . . ."

"You thought that I was a member of the Royal Canadian Mounted Police, didn't you?"

"Yes," nodded the boy, "that's what I thought."

"Well, I am," said Corporal Zachariah Denny.

CHAPTER TWO

Following the River

THE silence which followed Zachariah Denny's announcement was finally broken by the muffled thud of burning wood as it settled in the ashes of the stove. Fear, anger, humiliation and discouragement passed in turn across the boy's white face. But he made no sound. Moving slowly, he seated himself on the box and leaned back against the rough log wall. A stick of wood which he was about to add to the fire fell from his hand to the floor and he did not attempt to pick it up.

Zack's grey-blue eyes watched him carefully. "I'm only telling you this, Kop-a, because I have to. I'm not trailing you. Get that out of your head."

"I'm not going with you," said the boy shortly, looking down at his hands. "I'm waiting for the mail sled."

"It'll be a long wait," observed Zack. "Jon won't get here for another two weeks."

"Two weeks?" Kop-a lifted his head, startled. "Why, they said . . ."

"Who said?" interrupted Zack quickly.

"Two trappers. They gave me a lift from Tobuk to the Forks. I snowshoed over here from the Forks. They said Jon Mitchen would be along any day and always stopped at this shelter. They said he took passengers."

"Sometimes he does, but your friends got the time wrong."

"They aren't my friends," replied the boy heatedly.

"Did those trappers call themselves Mat and Joe Michaud and do they live about thirty miles up the river from here?"

"Yes."

"I'd like to know how much those men charged to take you from Tobuk to Grapevine Forks."

A sudden spasm of coughing seized Kop-a as he bent over to pick up the stick of wood on the floor. It was some moments before he could speak.

"They asked plenty," he answered finally, his voice thick, "but I had to get here."

"What in the devil are you doing here alone in the Arctic?" broke out Zack in exasperation. "I don't think you realize what you're up against!"

"I know, all right," answered Kop-a, looking up at Zack. His face, white and strained, gave proof of his words. But his eyes held a stubborn light of determination.

"I imagine Mat and Joe relieved you of a few of your supplies and probably charged you more than they agreed," said Zack casually, pulling a jackknife from his pocket.

Kop-a's face flushed angrily. "It happens that they did. You seem to know a lot about my affairs."

"No, but I know a lot about Mat and Joe. It's part of my job to know about people. Would you like to hear what I know about you?"

Kop-a did not answer. But there was a hint of fear

in his eyes as he looked up at Zack Denny, who had begun to whittle a piece of wood with the jackknife. Without waiting for the boy to object, he began to talk in ordinary conversational tones.

"Your name isn't Kop-a." The boy straightened sharply, his eyes indignant, but Zack hurried on. "You come from Outside and you've got a good American name. You've only been in the Arctic a few weeks. That parka, those trousers, your snowshoes, your whole outfit came from the Arctic, though. They were very well chosen and expertly made, probably by Eskimos along the coast farther west. The skins were caught in August because they don't shed. These things were sent to you, perhaps. You've had a good home, probably in the middle west." Zack's eyes searched the boy's face briefly and then returned to his whittling. "You've had plenty of money to spend but I don't think you've been very happy. . . . You like music. . . . Your greatest fear is that someone is searching for you through the Mounted Police. You're not a criminal but you feel hunted and you act it. You wish to go farther north or you wouldn't be waiting for Jon Mitchen who goes up as far as Lead River. I don't know why you're so determined to get north. It seems to be a life and death matter. And probably you'll get there if someone in the States doesn't stop you. Someone in the middle west." Zack now gazed directly at Kop-a who was sitting forward, staring at him with fascinated eyes. The knuckles of his hand, as it clutched the stick of wood, showed white.

"Nothing to worry over," and Zack smiled suddenly,

showing firm healthy teeth. "I just mentioned middle west because of your accent. Remember, I am not following you and I never heard of you before. The Mounted Police are not a bloodthirsty lot . . . we don't persecute. This happens to be one of my old patrols and for a certain reason I'm not in uniform. I'm just like the rest of the natives," and he pointed at his own parka and fur trousers which hung beside Kop-a's. "Do you know much about the Mounted Police?"

Kop-a's hand had relaxed its grip on the stick of wood. "I've seen them drill in Regina."

"You're smart enough," observed Zack frankly. "I imagine you're a pretty decent chap when you want to let down the bars. When was the last time you had a good laugh?"

The boy did not seem at all surprised by the question and regarded Zack soberly out of his dark eyes. "I can't remember," he answered slowly after a pause. "I can't remember but it must have been a long time ago."

"When you accomplish your errand, whatever it is, do you think you'll be able to laugh once in a while?"

"Oh, yes," and the set lines about the young mouth softened, "but not until I do accomplish it."

Zack threw away the stick of wood he had been whittling and closed his knife. "Now let's talk sense, Kop-a. You have a bad cold and you're out of food. I give you my word that I am not trying to hoodwink you or follow you. You have the word of a Mounted Police corporal. Does that mean anything to you? Unless I see you breaking the law or hear anything criminal against you, I shall leave you and your affairs alone. I won't ask you any questions. But you can't stay here. You've got to come along with me to Henry's. Then you can go where you please."

Kop-a remained silent for a moment. When he spoke his voice was quiet. "I'm staying here. You tricked me a few minutes ago the way you put that question about the Mounted Police."

"I had to make you talk," replied Zack earnestly. "It was either make you talk or take you out with handcuffs on." The corporal's grey-blue eyes looked directly at the boy. There was something clean and undeniably straightforward about this man. He spoke with assurance and his whole bearing gave evidence of right living and vitality. "Won't you take the word of a member of the Force?"

"But how am I to know you are a member of the Force? I'd be an awful fool to go traveling along with a stranger who might interfere with my plans. No, I'm staying here."

Zack rose to his feet swiftly. "Push that grub box over here and get me some wood before the fire goes out."

Taken by surprise, the boy obeyed mechanically and as if in spite of himself.

"While you eat, I'll try to find some wood to replace what we've burned. It's the law of the country. And I'll make some cocoa for us to drink this noon on the trail. Dig down among those tins and find a skillet and put it over the fire. Wait a minute and I'll give you a piece of fat to burn. Start up those flames. . . . Here, now, fry yourself some caribou. There isn't any choice in this matter, my boy. You're coming with me either with or without handcuffs and I hope it's without. I don't want you falling down from hunger on the trail. And I don't want to see you stay here and commit suicide. Let's say no more about it. When the cocoa's hot, pour it in that thermos. It's luck for you that I came along. Just get going."

There was distrust in Kop-a's brooding face. He hesitated as though still clinging to a dim hope that he might remain in the cabin. Zack took down the dogs' harnesses from the wall and looked back once more at the boy.

"Be ready in half an hour, Kop-a."

The door closed and it was a few moments before Kop-a moved. Then he put the caribou meat into the hot skillet. While it fried, he folded up his sleeping bag.

Half an hour later, Zack Denny drove his seven dogs and hoop-handled sled up to the door of the cabin. Kop-a, in mukluks, parka and fur-trimmed cap stood in the doorway with snowshoes and pack. His expression was not happy as he helped to load the sled and lash down covers over the packs. Then Zack motioned him to sit in the seat at the rear end of the sled and covered him with a heavy bear robe.

"Better keep warm and get over that cold," he advised. "Later you can help me, perhaps."

Kop-a nodded briefly. He sat listlessly, his head forward. A few minutes later, however, he gazed appraisingly at the dogs and at the sled in which he rode.

Zack, his face rimmed in wolverine, stood balanced upon the back of the runners with whip in hand. A brindle husky whined uneasily and pulled at her breastplate while Moise turned his head and watched Zack for a signal.

"Mush!" cried Zack suddenly.

There was a sharp crack of the long whip. The lash struck the snow in little spurts of white and the sled jerked forward to the jangle of its bell.

"We're going by the river," called Zack. "There's an errand I want to do and it will be easier on the dogs."

The dogs appeared healthy and well fed; their coats were thick and their legs moved sturdily in rhythm. In his driving Zack often called them by name. "Haw, Moise! Steady, Nig! Haw, Lingo and King! Speed up there, Barry! After him, Susie! Mush, Brindy!" There were long moments when he did not speak at all and the dogs forged ahead in a straight line. But it was difficult pulling, for the snow was soft and wet. Fortunately, the distance to the river was not long. Down a gentle incline and Zack halted the team that he might gaze upstream.

The wind had swept the river free of snow. But a blue mist, forced up through the lung holes of heavy ice, lay over its exposed surface and the air was damp and penetrating.

"We'll follow as far as we can," said Zack to the boy sitting in front of him. "But keep covered. This air is pretty raw."

The journey continued. Following the river was a new experience to Kop-a and unconsciously his face expressed pleasure as the runners skimmed noiselessly and lightly over the smooth surface. They were making good time when a blast of wind from the north met them at the first bend of the stream facing a long level stretch. Dogs and sled were swept broadside into a bank of willows, scrub growth and snow, despite their efforts to keep to the course. Brindy squealed loudly as she slipped and the whole team strove frantically to dig their claws into the ice. Zack yelled encouragement and pushed at the handle until the sled was righted and the dogs quieted. With a concentrated effort, the curve was passed. Kop-a, forgetting to keep covered, found himself sitting bolt upright, his body rigid and straining with the dogs. He felt Zack's eyes upon him as he settled back in his seat once more.

"I forgot that bend," said Zack. "It's some time since I've been up this river."

That the dogs loved their master was evident in the way they turned their heads and looked back at him, ever seeking his approval. Barry, the third dog, was a big grey puppy who fairly smiled at times, his long tongue hanging out and his lips curling upward. He was the largest of all the huskies and the most amiable. Susie, a smallish white dog with a brown ear, was just behind Barry and considered it her duty to keep him going. She snapped and scolded at his heels whenever he lessened his pace and it was apparent Susie had been placed there for that purpose.

"Mush, Barry," Zack would call. "Susie, keep after him! Susie is Barry's mother," explained Zack to Kop-a. "She won't let him grow up and still washes his face."

Once the dogs spied a white hare crossing the river some distance ahead. Brindy screamed shrilly and Moise whipped into instant action. The sled lurched, spun about at right angles, and nearly spilled as the dogs attempted to follow the hare into the brush. This time Zack applied the brakes. Saw teeth scraped the ice, and the dogs, panting and quivering, stood at attention, their faces guilty as Zack examined the load to see if it was secure.

"I ought to whip them for that," said Zack, "but I spend so many hours alone with them, they don't seem like dogs to me any more. And they know it, the little devils!"

The sun was now high in the heavens and Kop-a knew that it must be noon. They had been gradually leaving the flat wind-swept country. Green spruce lined the gullies which ran to the river from between rolling hills. Birch and cottonwood appeared and over to the west was the faint promise of mountain peaks. Now and then they passed a deserted cabin. Once there were fresh tracks of a fox crossing the river. But Zack pressed on until he came to a small hollow sheltered by trees. He halted the dogs and tied Moise to a stump.

"It's time to eat. I'm tying them up because if they should see another hare, we might have to finish the trip without them. We're behind schedule, so we won't stop long."

Kop-a seated himself on the edge of the sled and unscrewed the thermos bottle while Zack hunted in the grub box for some hardtack.

"You have some fine dogs," said Kop-a suddenly.

"I've had them since they were pups."

"Your sled is different, too," commented Kop-a.

Zack smiled, pleased with the boy's observations. "It was built for me at Cape North. Those runners are of Siberian hardwood, each runner a single piece steamed into shape. The hoop handle was invented by an Eskimo friend of mine."

The cocoa, made of powdered milk and chocolate, was steaming hot and the boy drank thirstily. Even the plain hardtack took on an unusually pleasant flavor. In spite of the damp air, Kop-a had not coughed to any extent and he appeared to be relaxed. Suddenly, in gazing about him, he caught sight of the dark outline of a cabin on the further turn of the river. Zack saw him staring and met his questioning look.

"No, that's not Henry's. That's Mat and Joe Michaud's cabin. I thought maybe we'd stop and collect what they owe you. They won't be too glad to see me, but I don't believe there'll be any trouble," and Zack tapped his parka on the right hand side. The slight gesture told Kop-a that he was wearing a pistol.

The boy looked startled for a moment and then an expression of grim satisfaction came into his face. "They won't be glad to see me either," he said as he finished his cocoa. "They charged me twenty dollars extra and took most of my bacon because we got into a sort of row."

"A row?"

"Yes," and Kop-a scowled as he talked. "Their dogs were left in harness all one night after a thirty-mile pull in soft snow. All because they got into an argument as to whose turn it was to cook the dog food. I fed the dogs some fish which I found in the grub box and it made them awfully mad. . . . The dogs cried in the night." Kop-a's eyes blazed angrily at the memory.

In spite of himself, Zack gave a faint chuckle as he packed the hardtack away. It was easy for him to imagine the whole scene . . . the two burly dark-skinned brothers wrangling while Kop-a, unseen in the night, fed the half famished beasts from their choicest supply of fish.

"This promises to be an interesting visit," Zack told himself as he untied Moise and prepared to start. "A most interesting visit!"

A few moments later, the sled sped over the ice toward the Michauds' cabin on the bend of the river.

CHAPTER THREE

A Stop at the Michauds' Cabin

TEN lean, ragged, ill-humored malamutes, separately staked, leaped and yelped at their chains as Zack tied his own team to a post in front of the Michaud cabin.

"If any of these dogs get loose, we'll have a fight on our hands," he shouted to Kop-a above the uproar. "Moise and King would like nothing better!" Zack paused as he saw the expression on the boy's face. "Well, Kop-a, you don't look exactly overjoyed at this visit!"

Kop-a's face was set. There was an expression of suffering as well as distaste in his dark eyes. He had caught a glimpse of two shadowy faces through the window of the cabin and he felt certain that Zack had seen them too. The faces had evaporated like misty phantoms but there remained with him the consciousness of being watched by small and evil eyes. Smoke curled upward from the tin chimney on the roof and snowshoes stood upright in a snow bank by the door. The Michaud brothers had evidently just returned from their trap lines, as the body of a red fox hung from a rope fastened to a high post just beyond the reach of the dogs.

"I'm not afraid of them," said Kop-a quickly. "It's just that I despise them. It makes me mad the way they treat their dogs," and he nodded his head in the direction of the yelping malamutes. "That grey one there," and he pointed at one dog which was lying down and not barking with the others, "he's old and they beat him all the time to make him run. Some day he'll just drop on the trail."

"I know how you feel," said Zack. "But for certain reasons, I can't do anything about the dogs to-day. Don't say too much," he warned, still watching Kop-a's face. "You'd better let me do the talking." As an afterthought he added, "There is some information I want and I know these two pretty well."

Kop-a made no reply. His eyes seemed to be searching expectantly for something as he looked to the left and the right of the cabin.

A sudden hush fell upon the dogs as Zack and Kop-a approached. It was a sinister silence in which one could almost hear the wind as it blew through the willows by the woodpile. The dead fox swung back and forth on its rope. Then there was a creaking sound of rusty hinges and the door of the cabin opened a few inches.

"Hello, Mat. Hello, Joe," said Zack.

There was no answer. The two brothers, one taller than the other, stood within. Because of the narrow opening, all that could be seen was a black sullen eye in each swarthy face.

"What'd yer want?" finally asked the shorter of the two. His voice was thick and guttural.

"Just passing by," replied Zack. "We're cold. Let us in."

"Let 'em in, Joe," said a higher voice and the taller

man backed away. "We ain't got nothin' to be ashamed of."

His brother moved away and the door swung open.

"Come on, Kop-a," said Zack under his breath.

Warm air, smelling of bacon fat, stale tobacco and drying wool greeted the newcomers. Mat and Joe had been about ready to eat their dinner, as various cans and bottles and two tin plates were laid out on a rough wooden table. The bacon was not in sight. Two caribou parkas hung by the door. Socks and mittens and woolen shirts hung on a line stretched behind a cast-iron stove. Except for the difference in height, Mat and Joe, with their straight black hair, looked just alike. Both wore greasy red sweaters, and fear smoldered in their eyes. Mat, more talkative than his brother, bore a deep scar on his cheek which drew up one side of his mouth when he talked, exposing a single yellow tooth.

"You ain't got nothin' on us."

There was a whining note in Mat's voice and the yellow tooth showed as high as the gum. Joe remained silent, his small weasel-like eyes alert. Once he turned his head swiftly and spat a long stream of tobacco juice in the direction of some firewood in a corner. Kop-a stood inside the door unnoticed as both men watched Zack.

"Where's Jean?" asked Zack, looking around.

Mat shifted his eyes for the fraction of a second. "You must-a knowed," he answered. "Jean's gone north for white fox."

"That so?" and Zack looked surprised.

Another pause followed. Joe pushed a piece of tobacco into his mouth and continued to watch Zack. Mat turned about and stooped to put more wood in the fire. There was the sound of crumpled paper.

"What have you got there?" asked Zack suddenly, pointing at the paper.

"Jest paper," answered Mat, hurriedly trying to push it into the stove.

"Let me see it." Zack stepped forward and pulled it out of Mat's hand. "Well, well, it looks like the paper that comes wrapped around bacon. One of the best brands. How long have you boys been using Swift's?"

"What'd yer say?" asked Mat, who was a little hard of hearing.

Zack repeated his question.

"We b'en usin' it a couple o' days now," answered Mat. "We made a trade wi' the young feller," and for the first time he shifted his eyes to Kop-a.

"A trade, eh?" and Zack stared at Joe. "What are you feeding your dogs these days, Joe? They're looking poor."

"They b'en sick," answered Joe slowly. "The flu got 'em. I feed 'em all right." He turned suddenly and pointed a dirty forefinger at Kop-a. "Wot you goin' ter do wi' 'im?" he asked Zack and there was a cunning look in his close-set eyes.

"Do with him? He's a friend of mine. Traveling with me."

"There's somethin' wrong wi' 'im," said Mat slyly. "'E din't register wi' the police at . . ."

"Close yer trap," shouted Joe at his brother fiercely.

Undaunted, Mat continued. "Yer always was a smart un, Denny. We knew somethin' was wrong wi' 'im an' yer hooked 'im first. Ole come by to-day. 'E said there was a stranger askin', quiet-like, down the river if a boy come up this way . . ."

"Hol' yer brayin'!" roared Joe, raising his arm as if to strike Mat, who subsided on a whining note, his mouth slightly open.

"I'm interested in just one thing now," said Zack. "You owe this boy twenty dollars and some bacon. Settle up and we'll get going."

" 'E stole our fish!" yelled Mat suddenly in a high voice. " 'E's a bad un an' we don' like 'im!"

"Your own dogs enjoyed the fish," replied Zack sharply and started to say more when Kop-a interrupted.

"I didn't steal your fish!" he denied indignantly. "I didn't eat one of them . . ." He stopped suddenly for there was a scratching sound behind the door at the rear of the cabin and the whimper of a dog could be heard. An eager look came into the boy's face and he made an obvious effort to control his voice when he spoke again. "I'll give you fifteen dollars for that puppy. You don't want him anyway. Then you'll owe me five. You can keep the bacon."

At this Mat's feelings gave way. "Get outer 'ere," he screamed, his voice shrill with rage. The scar on his cheek remained livid in his red face. "We've 'ad nothin' but trouble since we met up wi' yer. Git outer 'ere, yer little dirty city brat!"

But Joe's short bulky body had spun about with surprising quickness, and he reached for a tin coffee can on a shelf over his head. Carefully he counted out four five-dollar bills and flung them down on the table. " 'Ere's yer money. But I ain't sellin' yer the pup. I'd wring 'is neck, I'd let 'im rot 'fore I'd sell 'im to yer. 'E's no good, but you can't 'ave 'im."

"Take your money and go outside," said Zack to the boy. "I'll be along soon."

Kop-a picked up the money. When he looked up again, his dark eyes rested in utter contempt upon the two brothers before him.

"I hope I get the chance someday," he said and his voice was surprisingly calm and measured, "to see the two of you stand all night harnessed to a sled . . ."

"Git outer 'ere," raged Mat, waving a ragged sweater sleeve.

". . . without anything to eat," continued the boy in the same measured tones.

"Git! Git!" Joe was now edging to one side where a gun stood against the wall.

"Don't move, Joe!" Zack's hand was in his pocket and Joe knew that he was being covered by a service pistol. "Not another step, Joe. Go outside, boy, you've said enough. Easy, Mat, easy."

There was a rasping noise of rusty hinges. Kop-a disappeared. And for a few moments there was no other sound than the cries of a puppy as he continued to scratch frantically at the shed door.

"That kid ain't named Kop-a," said Joe, breaking the silence. " 'E ain't no Eskimo. Mat's right fer onc't. Yer gittin' a big reward fer 'im and 'e don't even know it. Yer smart, Denny."

"Thanks," said Zack coolly and studied the two swarthy brothers. "Where's Jean?" he asked brusquely.

"We tole yer," whined Mat. " 'E's gone fer fox." Mat was trying to warm his feet, which were abnormally large, in the oven.

"You going, too?" asked Zack.

"Naw, we like it 'ere."

Zack's eyes roved about him. The two brothers were comfortable enough. They had evidently just purchased a new primus stove and blankets. The Corporal glanced above at a shelf over the back door and then his gaze rested once more on the Michaud brothers. The puppy in the shed had stopped crying and could be heard digging in a corner.

"You'd better give me that other slab of bacon, Joe. It's up there on the shelf."

Joe hesitated, thought better of it, and finally gave Zack the bacon which he tucked under one arm.

"And now you get busy and cook some dog feed, Joe. Feed those dogs well for the next few days. I'll be coming through again soon and you know I'm fussy when it comes to dogs. Let that old grey one rest and don't forget the pup in there. No half rations . . . you're well stocked. If you don't like that pup, why don't you sell him?"

" 'E's ugly. 'E growls an' sulks. Jest like the brat," and Joe motioned towards the door through which Kop-a had gone. "We gotter train 'im."

"H'm. Well, keep him in good condition. I'll be seeing you again," and Zack slammed the door behind him.

As he went down the narrow snow path, his face sober and thoughtful, Zack held up the slab of bacon so that Kop-a, waiting on the sled, might see it.

"Thanks," said Kop-a. His voice was grateful but his eyes were watching the cabin. Zack slipped the bacon into the grub box and then untied the snubbing line which held Moise.

"No, they won't shoot at me," said the Corporal as he followed Kop-a's gaze. "They're yellow and it takes real nerve to shoot a policeman these days. Quiet, Moise! All set, Kop-a?"

"All set," answered the boy in a low voice.

"I'm sorry you couldn't buy the pup. Maybe you'll feel better when I tell you that it is only a question of time before the Police will take those dogs. A friend of mine has been watching them and there have been other complaints besides yours."

Kop-a looked around and his expression brightened for an instant. "That's good," he said. Then a sudden flash of distrust crossed his face. "Does your friend belong to the Force?"

"Yes, Sergeant Cunningham," answered Zack.

The boy made no reply but turned away and pulled the hood closer over his face.

Before the sled reached the lake, Zack and Kop-a passed through their first overflow. Water, which was from three to four inches deep, had been forced to the surface through airholes because of the river's solid freezing. The ice beneath the water was extremely slippery and the dogs moved slowly.

"If one of the dogs should slip," said Zack, "you'll

see him stop when he reaches dry ice and lap the water from his body. Nobody ever taught him that; he just knows it. A man has to learn through bitter experience that if he gets wet feet, he'd better stop immediately and build a fire before his feet freeze. Wet feet are dangerous things in the Arctic."

Kop-a seemed to be listening but Zack was not certain. Frequently the boy would turn his head and look back as they rounded each bend.

"Were you expecting Mat and Joe to follow?" Zack finally asked.

Kop-a appeared startled. "No, I hadn't thought of that. Why should they follow us?"

"Mat and Joe seem to think there's a reward being offered for you. They might follow as far as Henry's to see if we part company."

"How far are we from Henry's?"

"Twelve miles as the crow flies. By the way, while you were with the Michauds, did you ever hear them speak of their brother Jean?"

"Yes." The boy paused thoughtfully. "They seemed to worry over him a lot, wondering when they were going to see him and if he was well. They didn't seem to be very sure where he was."

"I see," said Zack.

Lone Tree Lake did not appear to be any different from the rest of the frozen white country, save for the dark fringe of trees which rimmed its edge. Night was fast shutting down. Surface water, lying in long shallow pools upon the lake ice, caught and held the blood-red reflection of the setting sun. Over in the east, like sentinels above the quiet tundra plains, reared jagged, splintered mountain peaks.

"You like the north?" asked Zack.

Kop-a nodded.

"I have learned to love it," said the young corporal.

A few moments later, they stopped for the last of their cocoa on the shore of the lake. "A month from now, you will begin to see green patches appear on the lower sides of those mountains," and Zack looked over to the east. Kop-a, sunk in heavy silence, raised his eyes and gazed absently at the mountains.

"The sun will feel warm on your back and the rivers will be full of floating ice," continued Zack. "Later on there will be anemones, buttercups, dandelions, violets, gold thread and, Heaven help us, mosquitoes. What's that?" he asked abruptly, following the direction of the boy's eyes as he looked back once more.

Something small and dark, scarcely more than a black dot against the snow, was following the tracks of the sled along the edge of the lake. There was a breathless moment of waiting.

"It's the puppy!" yelled Kop-a suddenly. "It's the puppy!"

With one leap, the boy cleared the sled and started down the lake, slipping, sliding, and calling to the puppy which came running to meet him.

CHAPTER FOUR

"Too Small for a Sled Dog"

LIKE a small black whirlwind, the yelping puppy cleared the distance, ending the run with a final leap into Kop-a's arms. From then on there was a frantic mixture of boy and dog. The boy slipped and sat down on the ice while the puppy, his high bark sounding sharply through the cold air, tore around him in frenzied circles of joy. Zack, holding his own dogs in check, waited silently as Kop-a finally approached with the small dog in his arms.

"He's wet!" announced Kop-a. "He must have waded that overflow. What shall I dry him with?"

Zack, remembering his recent lecture on the horrors of wet feet in the Arctic, smiled to himself. The boy was an apt pupil. "Here," he said, reaching into the sled bag which hung from the handle bars and pulling out a white cotton storm shirt, "use this."

The small dog, heavily furred in coal black except for a white tail and white ear, gazed up at Zack out of fierce puppy eyes, the thick ruff on his neck encircling his head like a wide collar. In his short life, he had known a single friend, the boy who now held him, and the world beyond was one of bitter enmity. Though exhausted, his mouth open and gasping for breath, his body was primed for battle, ready to spring should

Zack come too near. A wavering growl sang in his throat.

"They've starved him . . . he's just a handful of fur," Kop-a exclaimed indignantly.

The expressions of both boy and dog were so much alike that for a moment Zack had a desire to laugh. Even Joe had remarked about the resemblance. "Jest like the brat," he had said.

"What are you going to do with him?" asked Zack as Kop-a seated himself on the edge of the sled and commenced to dry the small animal with the shirt.

"Do with him? Keep him!" The boy's eyes were stormy as he looked up at Zack. "He belongs to me now. Of course, if I have to . . ." He weighed his words anxiously and carefully. "I'll give him to some person who'll be kind to him. But I don't want him to go back to that place again! Mat and Joe don't like him. He's too small for a sled dog. They won him in a game of cards and he was thrown in with some skins as a prize. It amuses them to make him growl. They want to break his spirit. Here, pup." Between rubs, he fed the small eager mouth a piece of chocolate from his pocket. Zack recognized the chocolate as some he had given the boy the day before.

"See, he's a nice little fellow," and Kop-a, forgetting his own troubles, became quite natural in his manner as he tried to exhibit and dry the puppy at the same time. All of Zack's dogs were watching the performance, their heads up and bodies tense. King was openly antagonistic.

"Keep him away from my dogs," warned Zack. "They're jealous."

"I know," answered the boy. "Quiet, pup," he scolded the wriggling body beneath the shirt. The puppy, his white ear cocked, continued to watch Zack guardedly as Kop-a proceeded to show his fine points.

"He's well shaped. Has a nice back . . . . it's straight and sturdy. When he cocks his ear, it means that he's ready to fight. And when his tail is dry, it curls over. He'll be all right as soon as he gets some decent food. He doesn't know how to play."

There was a pleading note in Kop-a's voice and the puppy, as though conscious of being appraised, began to watch Zack anxiously. Again Zack was struck by their similarity. The dog registered the boy's emotions so perfectly that Kop-a seemed to talk for them both.

Zack stared more carefully. The black fur on the puppy's flanks had frozen in string-like shreds and was matted close to his thin little body. Kop-a rubbed vigorously, talking the while. It was then that Zack noticed that the dog balanced on three legs and held a fore paw in the air.

"What's wrong with his paw?"

"Nothing," answered the boy. Suddenly he paused. "Why, it's bleeding," he exclaimed. "What do you suppose happened to it?"

"Sharp ice, maybe," said Zack, leaning closer. "That was a hard trip for a puppy to make. Stop your growling, young feller, I'm not going to touch you. Roll him up and keep him warm, Kop-a. You know, don't you, that it's a serious thing to steal another man's dog in this country?"

Kop-a looked up in quick concern and the puppy peered out of his white wrappings anxiously.

"I didn't steal him," objected the boy. "He just followed."

"Did you know he was going to follow?"

"I hoped so," answered the boy frankly. "There was a rotten board in the floor of the shed and while I was waiting for you, I crawled under and loosened it a bit."

"Well, I'll be darned!" said Zack. "So that's what I heard." There was a pause in which Zack seemed lost in thought. The boy and the dog waited, their eyes upon him.

"Kop-a," said Zack finally, "I promised not to ask you any questions and I mean to keep my word. So it will be up to you to decide what we shall do next. We'll go ahead to Henry's . . . or we'll go back to the Michauds' with the dog." Kop-a started to speak but Zack continued. "It is possible that I could persuade them to let you buy this puppy, but I doubt it. And there's another angle which you must consider. Mat and Joe have heard something about you from Ole Starnes, a trapper. I gather there is someone south of here making inquiries about you. Possibly there is a notice about you in the Gazette. As I'm not traveling with you under arrest, it is likely that Mat and Joe will follow, waiting to pick you up as soon as my back is turned. If there is a reward, they'll want it and they won't leave a stone unturned. Losing the puppy doesn't make them like us any better, you understand. They may follow on the pretext of recovering him. Shall we take the dog back, giving them less reason to follow or shall we go ahead? You'll have to decide."

There was a long moment of silence. The boy sat

with his head bowed and the small dog, as if sensing a dilemma, moved closer and rested his chin on Kop-a's fur mitten.

"I couldn't do it," said the boy at last looking up at Zack. "I couldn't do it," he repeated. "They'd beat him . . . they'd kill him. I'm the only friend he has."

"Let's go ahead," said Zack quickly.

In the three hours which followed, the dogs and sled wove in and out along the edge of the long frozen lake and then climbed westward through a forest of young spruce. At the edge of the forest, Zack stopped unexpectedly beside a small cabin. Though night had fallen, the moon was full and shone brightly on the snow with a greenish cast. Branches of spruce, ridged with snow, glittered frostily.

"I lived here for a while," said Zack, giving Kop-a the dogs' reins to hold. "It was at the end of my patrol and the Henrys named it Denny's Mountain. I like this old cabin," and he disappeared inside. When he finally emerged, he was carrying a load of firewood in his arms. With a rope, he lashed the wood securely to the sled, making no explanations.

"No one's stopped here all winter," he announced, "except the squirrels. Did you ever hear Mat complain about his 'cold feets' when you traveled with them?"

"Yes, his feet were always cold. They're awfully big, too."

Zack chuckled. "We're almost at the Henrys' now. See that light down there?"

Kop-a leaned forward. In spite of hunger and weariness, he was not unaware of the beauty before him. Hill after hill, rolling gently, a sea of white billowing waves, stretched endlessly ahead. Forests of spruce shadowed the valleys, while the top of each hill gleamed silver beneath the moon. A single light shone in the distance, the only sign of human habitation. From the distance came the barking of a dog.

"That's one of E. B.'s dogs," said Zack in a hushed voice. "They're fine folks," he added. "They've lived in this valley for twenty years. Everyone calls Mr. Henry 'E. B.' . . . even his wife." The dogs, resting, got to their feet as Zack balanced himself once more on the runners.

"Mush, Moise! You know where you are now! Haw, King! Onto your job, Susie, after Barry!" The braided whip, cracked by a deft twist of the wrist, snaked and coiled along the snow. The weary dogs started, lagging somewhat in their efforts. "Almost there, now," called Zack encouragingly.

At the bottom of the hill, Zack stopped to examine a trap. "Nothing in it," he reported. "Guess Mrs. Henry came here to-day. Looks like the print of her snowshoes."

"Does Mrs. Henry look after traps?" asked Kop-a curiously.

"I'll say she does," answered Zack with a chuckle. "Wait till you see her. She can shoot better than any man around here. Except E. B. Shot a bear once when it walked into her kitchen. The skin's on her bedroom floor now. Ask her to show it to you. She can paint pictures, drive a dog team, build a snowhouse and swing an axe. Wears deerskin trousers most of the time and studies the fashion magazines by the hour to keep up with the styles. Gets all kinds of mail from people who have stayed at the house. Letters from miners, explorers, herders, missionaries. Everyone likes her. She took care of me when I hurt my leg last spring. But if I start talking about Mrs. Henry, we'll never get there. Mush, dogs, mush!"

As the lights of the Henrys' home grew brighter from the top of each hill, the dogs ceased to lag and ran with fresh impetus. On the slope of the final hill they became difficult to manage. The sled, gathering momentum, almost exceeded their speed, knocking against the hind legs of the rear dogs, and Zack was forced to use his brake. Faster, faster, raced the dogs. Suddenly two dark buildings and some outlying sheds came into view, but the dogs dashed ahead, seeming to know the way. Past the lighted house . . . on to a large square building with an open door. And then with a final burst of speed, Zack shouting, the sled bell jangling, the dogs barking, the sled entered the barn in a rush, the entire team coming up against a stall in a heap. Dogs from the adjoining stalls set up a cry. In the midst of the uproar, a door opened at the farther end of the barn and a lantern appeared.

"That you, Zack?" called a cheery voice.

"Hello, E. B.!" answered Zack. "We made our usual entrance, didn't we?"

"Sounded like old times," said E. B., coming nearer. "Where you headed for? How long can you stop with us?"

"I'm going straight north. Ought to leave in the morning."

Gradually the barking stopped. There was a second figure behind E. B. carrying a huge kettle.

"Hi, Raven!" called Zack. "Always ready with the dog feed, aren't you?"

An Eskimo, smiling broadly, nodded his head.

"Mother's been watching for you all afternoon," said E. B., spreading some pans in a row on a bench. Suddenly he looked up. Kop-a stood at his side with the puppy in his arms.

"For Pete's sake, where did you come from?" exclaimed E. B. in surprise. "I didn't know you had a passenger," he said to Zack.

"This dog is hungry," said Kop-a. "Can he have his now?"

"Sure, sure," answered E. B. heartily, and with a ladle he dipped some warm corn meal mush and meat into one of the pans. The puppy, his whole body shaking with excitement, ate convulsively, with a gulping sound.

"Well, he is hungry," observed the man. "Where you from, son?"

"Grapevine Forks," answered the boy.

"Anyone going north from here in a few days?" asked Zack, finally appearing from one of the stalls.

"No one until Jon Mitchen comes along," answered E. B. "Didn't you say you were going north, Zack?"

"Yes, but this boy might want to rest a few days; I don't know. I think that puppy's had enough for the first time, Kop-a. Put him in the stall with Barry. And shut the door when you come out. Barry will be good to him. He's a puppy himself. My! it's nice to see you, E. B.! Don't tell me you're a little fatter." Zack grinned down at E. B. who came only to his shoulder and appeared to be a plump ball of fur in the lantern's light.

"Well, you know Mother's cooking, my boy. It can do a lot of damage. She's got dinner all ready in there now. Your letter came yesterday morning and Raven couldn't wait to go out onto the tundra and get a swan. She's baked it. Made a blueberry pie, too, in your honor. We've missed you, Zack," said the older man with feeling.

"Maybe I'm not glad to get here!" and Zack took a deep breath. "Come on, Kop-a, it's mug-up! Two of the sweetest words in the Arctic dictionary. It means 'eat!' " Zack turned and waited for Kop-a who was fastening the door of the stall. "Raven will finish feeding the rest of the dogs and see that everything is all right."

E. B. was holding the lantern above Zack's sled. "We'll unload you after supper, Zack. But what are you carting wood around for?" he asked, peering at the firewood lashed with ropes. "I never knew you to travel with wood before."

"I got it out of my cabin as I came along," answered Zack. "Whoever occupies that cabin to-night will have to cut his own wood to keep warm."

"You being followed, Zack?" asked E. B. quickly.

"Wouldn't surprise me at all," replied the young corporal.

CHAPTER FIVE

Evening at the Henrys' Roadhouse

Mrs. Henry was a tall, rangy woman with intelligent blue eyes beneath her iron-grey hair. As a festive touch for the occasion, she was wearing a neat brown-and-white-checked gingham dress with apron to match. Her moccasined feet made no noise as she crossed the long room and she walked with a buoyancy which told of a life in the out-of-doors, of long treks in winter snows and spring rains. Her fresh ruddy face beamed with welcome as she reached up to the young officer, a bit taller than herself, and kissed him heartily on both cheeks.

"Zack! I thought you'd never come! How are you and is the leg well now? You don't seem to be limping and you've put on some weight!" she exclaimed, holding him off at arms' length.

"I'm fine, Mrs. Henry, thanks to your good nursing! It's wonderful to see you again! The dogs raced on that last mile, but even then it seemed a long one."

"Are your feet dry? Here, let me help you off with that parka."

Then Mrs. Henry caught sight of Kop-a. He was standing just inside the doorway, looking about him quietly, his hood pushed back. "Why, Zack, who is this?" she asked in surprise.

"Friend of mine named Kop-a. Got a bed for him?"

"Of course," said Mrs. Henry. "But I'll have to put him in one of the bunks in your room. The roof leaks in the south room and E. B. hasn't had time to mend it." As she spoke, she scanned Kop-a's face intently. The warm indoor air made him cough suddenly and a look of concern crossed her face. "E. B.," she called, "help the boy off with his things and put both the parkas out in the entry. Raven will beat them later. Raven," addressing the Eskimo who had just entered, "serve the soup and we'll sit down." Mrs. Henry, with her usual efficiency, swung into action.

Zack, with his outer wraps and mukluks removed and a pair of E. B.'s moccasins on his feet, stood looking about him happily. A gasoline lamp hanging from the ceiling lighted every corner. He loved this big room with its roughhewn beams, red curtains, and braided rugs with crimson borders. Mrs. Henry had spared no effort to add beauty as well as comfort to her home and the room gleamed with a brightness and warmth in sharp contrast to the grey Arctic twilight outside. A huge cast-iron stove radiated heat at one end. Close by was a long dining table with chairs. At the other end of the room was a counter laden with gay woolen blankets, hunting shirts, mukluks, snow glasses, lanterns, primus stoves, dog harnesses, thermos bottles, knives. On the wall in back steel traps hung by chains in heavy clusters.

The Henrys' home was not only a roadhouse but also a store, and the largest building of its kind for miles around. Most of the lumber had been brought north by mining prospectors and the miners, departing, had left the barren structure for the next newcomer. Mr. and Mrs. Henry had lost no time in transforming the dingy building into a home. Cotton cloth and paint of gay colors had worked wonders. Running a small country store, trading merchandise for skins with native trappers, substituting as mail carrier and acting as guide for hunting parties, Mr. Henry had made a comfortable living. Mrs. Henry, capable and active, had run her own trap lines, planted gardens, canned vegetables and fruits in the short summer months, and had taken in travelers who had come that way. For twenty years she and her husband had combined their courage, brain and brawn and had prospered, winning the esteem and love of all who knew them.

"You have a new bench!" exclaimed Zack, spying a rustic seat at one side of the stove.

"An old wreck washed up off Cape Evans," explained Mrs. Henry, "and some natives traded the timber for cloth. Are you going to the coast, Zack, or are you as usual unable to talk about your plans?"

"I'm aiming that way," said Zack and then stopped short upon seeing Kop-a. For the first time, the boy had removed his brown knit cap with the fur ear laps, and seeing him without it gave Zack a slight start of surprise. Kop-a's hair was blond, a decided straw color and a striking contrast to his dark eyes and brows. This alone belied Eskimo blood. His head was well shaped, the nose straight, his mouth and chin clean cut. He carried himself with a poise and an aloofness beyond his years.

Apparently a carefree life of laughter and play had not been his. He was thin, too . . . slender as a birch in his flannel shirt and long deerskin trousers.

"Copper . . . Copper . . ." Mrs. Henry also gazed at the boy who was bending over the counter of knives, beyond the reach of her lowered voice. "I've heard that name around here, Zack. And it seems to me as if I've seen him somewhere before. I'm trying to think . . ."

"Try and place him if you can," said Zack earnestly, his own voice lowered. "It would be doing me a great favor. I found him alone down near Grapevine Forks. He spells his name K-o-p-a. As you know, all white men going north sign up with the police for protection. If they're not heard from for a while, the police investigate. Evidently this boy slipped through in some way. He'd never get by traveling alone. Also, according to Mat and Joe Michaud, some one is hunting for him. All this makes me think he's a runaway. I told the Michauds he was a friend of mine and pretended not to be interested in their story. But I am. In a way, it puts me on the spot to be helping a runaway boy but I rather like the youngster. If I can help him, I will. I certainly don't want him to fall into the hands of the Michauds for reward money. Were you tuned in to the radio station at Aklavik this afternoon? And is E. B.'s transmitter working?"

"I heard all the announcements but there was no news about a missing boy. And E. B.'s transformer burned out last week. He's sending to Seattle for a new one. Aren't you carrying your two-way?"

"Not this trip. Well, it's a lucky break for the boy. There's no way of checking up on him. But I think he'd confide in you, if he had the chance."

"Maybe," said Mrs. Henry, her voice doubtful. "Anyone can tell, though, that he has a mind of his own. I'll see what I can do," she added hastily, as E. B. and Kop-a left the counter and came towards them. At this moment Raven entered, bearing four steaming bowls of soup on a tray. From the kitchen came a loud sizzling noise and the appetizing odors of a dinner cooking.

"Everyone come over here," called Mrs. Henry cheerily,. leading the way to the table. "Kop-a, you sit right next to Mr. Henry where he can keep an eye on your plate. Zack, take your old place with your back to the fire. This soup will be good for that cold, son," she said, looking at Kop-a. "If you'll stay with us for a while, I'll guarantee to cure that cold."

"It's very kind of you," replied the boy politely but hurriedly, "but I shall have to go along as soon as possible."

"How far you going?" asked E. B.

"To the coast," replied Kop-a briefly.

His manner was calm enough but the hand which picked up a cracker was nervous and unsteady. Mrs. Henry's eyes met Zack's for an instant. There was a look of compassion in their blue depths as she leaned forward and pushed the bowl of soup nearer the boy.

"Eat while it's hot, son. I imagine you've come a long way already. But you must eat and keep well if you wish to reach the coast. It's a long hard pull."

There was a flash of gratitude in Kop-a's dark eyes as he looked back at her. Her interest and thoughtful concern touched him. And gradually his defensive attitude became lost in the friendly atmosphere, his manner less tense and cautious. As he finished his soup, his eyes strayed now and then to this woman who seemed so friendly.

In the beginning, Kop-a ate moderately. But the golden-brown stuffed swan, wild currant jelly, salted greens and freshly baked bread generously spread with butter seemed to break down his reserve. He ate in a half-famished manner, making no conversation, his eyes glancing from one speaker to another.

"What's the news down north?" asked Zack when the huge frame of the swan, minus legs, wings and breast, had been removed from the table by Raven and they were waiting for the blueberry pie.

"Well," said E. B., "everything's the same in many ways. The trappers did well with their fox this year. A small school of white whales was killed last year and that supply brought the people through half of the winter. This spring, they're counting on the walrus. I heard Mary telling you about the wreck off the Cape. And of course the whole coast has been stirred up over the reindeer trouble. Raven here," and E. B. nodded his head in the direction of the Eskimo who had entered with the pie, "knows your friend Lucas Joules very well. Lucas has had a lot of hard luck."

"You know Lucas Joules?" asked Zack of Raven.

A spoon clattered noisily against a plate as though it had been hastily dropped. Immediately all of Zack's trained instincts were aroused but he did not move his gaze from Raven's face.

"Lucas good friend," replied the Eskimo, placing the pie before Mrs. Henry.

"Who . . . what name did you say?" asked Kop-a as though the words were forced from him. Zack now turned his head in time to see Kop-a staring wide-eyed at Raven. A spoon lay where it had fallen on the edge of the plate.

"Joules, Lucas Joules," answered E. B. "He comes from an old Alaskan family. One of the finest Eskimos I have ever met. Do you know him?"

Kop-a made no reply but continued to stare at Raven. Then, conscious that all were watching him, he lowered his eyes, his face slightly flushed.

"Lucas Joules is one of the finest herders on the coast," offered Mrs. Henry, filling the pause which followed as she cut the pie into five even sections. "He would no more rustle reindeer and change their earmarks than I would. Lucas is being framed!"

"No doubt about it," agreed her husband. "Have you heard much talk about it, Zack?"

"Only a few rumors. Tell me what you know."

"Well, to begin with, Lucas has had a lot of so-called hard luck. But I'm wondering . . . You know, he's Buckley's top hand. Last spring some of the herds stampeded toward the sea for salt and Buckley lost a good many fawns. No one knows what caused the stampede. Year before, Lucas' herd boys left in a body without saying good-bye. The herds went wild after mushrooms and the rustlers helped themselves to the deer. Now who started all this commotion? Deer as a rule are contented on their own ranges with moss and water. The warble flies weren't any worse than usual.

"Of course these native herders are jealous of Lucas, who comes from a long line of chiefs and has an unusually good education. He's been Outside, you know. There are a few native herders who'd like to have Lucas arrested and an investigation made because some of their deer were found in the Buckley herds with the earmarks cut over . . . one of the lowest tricks among herders."

"Where has Buckley been all this time?" asked Zack. Kop-a was quiet now, his eyes on E. B.

"Buckley isn't around much. It's Lucas who is really running the ranch. Paul Buckley's interests are in archaeology on Saint Lawrence Island. The latest news is that he's fed up with all this trouble and wants to sell out."

"He isn't at the ranch half the time," sputtered Mrs. Henry. "And what he sees in digging up old pots and pans and decayed bones on a frozen island is more than I can understand. Why, they say . . ."

"Now, Mary," interrupted E. B. laughing, "you know it isn't as bad as that. Buckley's a fine man. He's been a bachelor all his life and is one of those crusty, quick-tempered people. When you once break through his shell he's all right. I think he's crusty because he's all wrapped up in his work and doesn't wish to be disturbed. By now it's a habit. He's obsessed with this bug of excavating. Seems he ranks high in his line of work, too. Last year the papers were full of how he found some of the oldest ivory in the country. It's now in some museum."

"I heard about it," said Zack.

"You see," continued E. B., "It was John Buckley who built up that business in the beginning. John was Paul's younger brother. John Buckley was a remarkable character. I guess there'll never be another John Buckley. He had great influence with the Eskimos. Sent the younger ones to Reindeer Stations for training and helped them to get launched with their own herds. The Eskimos fairly idolized him. But John died about three years ago. He overworked. And I guess it just about broke Paul Buckley's heart. There were just two things that Paul loved and they were his young brother John and his own work. Well, Paul took over the reindeer business automatically but he has no interest in it. I rather pity him. It's hard to be in two places at the same time."

"How'd he happen to find Lucas?"

"It's quite a story. When John Buckley first came north, he hired a man named Andre Angola. Lucas at that time was working on a freight boat packing meat. He discovered Andre Angola selling Buckley's meat on the side and feathering his own nest. Buckley was tipped off and Angola was fired. Disappeared into thin air . . . he was a queer one, they say. Then Buckley began to notice Lucas. Liked him and sent him to a training school and made him top hand. When Paul took over, Lucas kept on being top hand."

"Wouldn't Paul Buckley put up a fight to protect

Lucas if necessary? He must appreciate him somewhat."

"Sure he would. But it would be an awful mess and banded together, those herders might put it over. And meanwhile, Lucas' reputation is getting a black eye. People who don't know the real circumstances are always ready to believe the worst. Lucas is proud . . . proud of his blood. And besides being accused of rustling, Lucas has had his labret stolen. It was made of jadeite, beautifully carved, and had been handed down through several generations. Lucas and his wife are heartbroken."

"You don't say!" exclaimed Zack indignantly. "That must be the labret he told me about when we were drifting out to sea on an ice floe. It was after I first met him. Our situation looked pretty serious and he made the remark he was sorry he had no children to leave the labret to. Antique dealers had been after it but he wouldn't sell. So that's the labret which was stolen!"

"That's the one," answered E. B. "Lucky for you two the Coast Guard boat spotted you, wasn't it?"

"Yes, God bless 'em. A fine bunch of men and I wish more people knew of the important work they are doing in the north. If it hadn't been for Lucas, who first saw me from his kayak, and the Coast Guard, I wouldn't be here eating blueberry pie."

Throughout the remainder of the meal, Zack was conscious of Kop-a's eyes studying him. When the meal was finished, all rose and seated themselves by the great stove, E. B. smoking his pipe and Mrs. Henry knitting, glancing over her needles at Kop-a who sat in the shadow. Her face wore a perplexed expression as if she were still trying to remember where she had seen him before.

"It seems only yesterday," said E. B., his mind still on the conversation, "that John Buckley started in with his reindeer. And now the herds graze from Slate River to the mountains! He had a fine influence on other herders because he was honest and gave full measure and a square deal. I'd hate to see some greedy corporation get in there and squeeze the Eskimos out.

"The reindeer industry is one of the finest things that could have come to the north," continued E. B. with enthusiasm. "It's teaching the Eskimo to be self-supporting, responsible and steady. White people have depleted his supply of whalebone, whale oil, ivory, oil and furs. He's got to live on what's left and that's mighty little these days. Only last week a young herder came through here. Used to be the shiftless roving type. Someone got him interested in reindeer and he trained at one of the stations. Now he and five other herders are working together. He's married and his wife and child help him out on the range. They have meat to eat and skins to wear. His whole life is changed."

"He's a fine young man," added Mrs. Henry. "Left us some fawnskins in payment for his lodging. I'm making them into shirts and socks."

"The day will come, I believe, when they will use the Iceland pony for rounding up the reindeer. It would save carrying dog food cross-country, as the pony eats practically the same food as the deer."

Zack nodded. "They're talking about it now."

"Some day," and Mrs. Henry spoke with determination, "I'm going to take my paint box and brushes down there. What a picture it would make . . . reindeer milling about in circles, their antlers turned back, corralled behind walls of ice, waiting to be counted. . . . Outside would be herdsmen's tents and strings of dogs and a sunset . . ."

"One of those lemon green and amethyst ones," suggested Zack.

"Exactly. And if only I could paint in the sounds . . . the clatter of their horns and hoofs!"

"Anyone would think that you'd been there already," remarked E. B. "But we'll make the trip some day, I promise you, Mary. . . ."

"I'll remind you of it now and then, E. B.," returned his wife.

"Something tells me, Zack," and E. B. gave a long puff of smoke, "that you're on your way down there. Like the rest of the Force, you wear a poker face when folks start asking questions. Training, I know. But be careful, lad. You're dealing with some clever crooks. The kind that put powder marks on your back. But as for Lucas' being a thief . . ."

"Rubbish!" snorted Mrs. Henry. "It just makes me piping mad to think about it. Lucas steal! Why, once when he stopped here, he discovered that E. B. had given him too much money in changing a bill. What did he do but drive back twenty miles in a storm to make it right. Lucas is as honest as the day is long!"

Mrs. Henry's ball of yarn streamed across the floor towards Kop-a, who stooped over, picked it up and brought it to her. She thanked him with a smile but noticed that he moved mechanically, as though barely realizing what he was doing. As Kop-a returned to his seat once more, facing the living room and Mrs. Henry, he drew in his breath sharply. The door leading to the kitchen had slowly opened. A small dark figure, walking upright with a shuffling motion, came through the door and crossed the lower half of the living room. As it approached the light in the middle of the room, Kop-a saw that it was a young dark-colored bear with a round protruding stomach and a shiny nose. The cub gave one hasty glance in the direction of Mrs. Henry and walked even faster to the front door. With a quick movement of his forepaw, he lifted the latch and disappeared into the night. The closing of the door caused the gasoline lamp to flicker and flare. Mrs. Henry looked up at the light and then at Kop-a, noting his startled expression.

"Did a little bear walk through here?" she asked.

Zack answered before the boy could speak. "Yes, he came right in the back door and went out the front. Another one of your orphans?"

"Oh, that's just Soapy. Soapy Smith. Raven must have forgotten to lock the back door." There was a note of despair in Mrs. Henry's voice. "I declare, that cub is the worst nuisance we've ever had. Yesterday he stole a whole cake and climbed to the roof of the barn with it, all the dogs yapping below. And there he sat grunting and chewing, his face all stuck up with marshmallow frosting. I hoped that it would make him good and sick, but it didn't. This is the first time he has dared to come into the house since. 'Fraid he'd get spanked."

"Where'd you find him? That's some name for a bear!" said Zack, laughing.

"Somebody shot his mother," answered E. B. "I found Soapy near her body, crying as if his heart would break. He came back day after day and gradually I made friends with him. I felt awfully sorry for him but I've been feeling sorry for myself ever since. I brought him home in a bag and he thinks he owns the place now. Comes and goes like a landlord. And he steals so expertly that we named him after that gold digger Soapy Smith of Alaska. But now I wish that somebody would take him to a nice zoo. At times I wouldn't even object if a little buckshot sent him flying . . ." E. B. spoke soberly but he winked an eye at Zack.

"You don't wish any such thing," said Mrs. Henry indignantly. "You're as softhearted as a baby when it comes to Soapy and you know it. You'd feel terrible if anything happened to him. He is a nuisance but when he crawls up into my lap and wants to be rocked, I declare I forget all the damage he's done. Last week he broke loose from the shed where he sleeps and climbed the rose ladder into Miss Simpkins' room. She's the missionary over at Horn Creek and one of our best customers. But I don't believe she'll ever come again. Soapy must have looked at least ten feet tall to her in the moonlight as he stood by the window examining one of her shoes. She let out a frightful yell and E. B. had to dress and put Soapy back in the shed. I expect he'll run off by himself when he's older."

The mystery of the bear explained, Kop-a was yawning, his eyes heavy with sleep. The day's trek had been a long one.

"Want to go to bed, young man?" Mrs. Henry asked.

But it was evident that Kop-a was reluctant to leave their company. With an obvious effort he straightened up and shook his head.

Mrs. Henry paid no attention. "Your bed's ready," she said quickly, "and to-morrow's another day. Now don't you two sit up all night talking. E. B., when you lock Soapy Smith in, stop by the woodpile and bring in more wood. And Zack, I'll be up early in case you decide to leave. But I think a day's rest would be awfully good for you. Come, son, I'll show you to your room."

As footsteps overhead grew fainter down the long hall, E. B.'s rotund figure leaned forward in his chair and he cleared his throat.

"Zack, who's meeting that boy, and where did he come from? He seems pretty young to be going to the coast alone. Is he under your care?"

"Not exactly, E. B. Up to the present time, he hasn't confided much in me. In fact, he has quite an aversion to the Force. Don't ask me why. I met him below here in a cabin waiting for Jon Mitchen. He is determined to reach the coast. I'm hoping Mrs. Henry will get him to talk."

"Has he ever been north before?"

"Apparently. I believe he knows more than he lets on. This afternoon, I saw him pick up the whip and give it a twist like an old timer. It's one of the first things a boy in the north learns to do. But I don't think he's ever been on a long trek before."

"Would you take him along with you if he asked to go?"

"I might, but I'm not hankering for the responsibility. On the other hand, I'd hate to see the youngster fall in with the wrong people . . ."

"Such as the people who might sleep in your cabin to-night?"

"Exactly."

"Oh, you policemen!" E. B. shook his head. "You're a great lot. I daresay you've a hundred theories all mapped out now about that boy. Of course, we'd like to have him stay here. Mary has already taken quite a fancy to him. But you say he's in a hurry. How are you aiming to go?"

"Through the Lost Lands."

E. B. whistled and remained silent for a little while. Then he said:

"Well, I suppose you know your own business best. Of course, I'm certain now you're headed for the reindeer country. But frankly, Zack, with all credit due you, I wish they'd sent an older man. Someone who knows that country and has been there before. Mosquitoes and bogs in summer. Squalls and tundra in winter. A hell on earth. And if you take him . . . a boy new to the trail . . . I wish you weren't going that way. Any day those lakes will begin to thaw . . . I don't like it . . . I don't like it. . . ."

CHAPTER SIX

Kop-a-noo

THE room formerly occupied by Zack was long and narrow with log walls peeled of their bark and a window looking southward. Lest he awaken Kop-a, Zack blew out his candle and stood motionless in the doorway for a few moments, waiting for his eyes to get adjusted to the darkness. The moon outside was screened by overhanging clouds. Deep shadows darkened the corners of the room but he could dimly see the figure of the boy lying in one of the lower bunks. And the sound of slow gentle breathing told that he was asleep.

Feeling his way carefully, Zack tiptoed through the narrow space toward his own bunk. Suddenly his foot struck something hard. The object rolled noisily across the floor and for a moment there was a pause in the steady breathing from the bunk. Then it became regular once more and Zack leaned forward. An empty cup . . . a hot drink for Kop-a . . . no doubt Mrs. Henry had heard him coughing and had gone downstairs to the kitchen. He remembered hearing someone in the outer room while he talked with E. B. He hoped that Kop-a had confided in her freely. Not only would Mrs. Henry strive to clarify the situation but it was plain that her interests and sympathies were with this young wandering stranger. A woman with a great heart. . . .

Zack stooped to pick up the cup and as he did so,

a wavering, high-pitched growl sounded in his ear. Startled, he straightened up and gazed into the round bright eyes of the puppy whose head barely showed over the top of the boy's sleeping bag. The one white ear was cocked forward . . . the puppy was primed for battle.

"Hello, you little beggar. So he brought you up here, did he?"

The puppy stared back, tense and challenging.

"Just alike, you two. Even greasy Joe Michaud recognized it."

With this thought of Joe, Zack reached for a key in his pocket, unlocked the padlock of his bag and drew out his binoculars. He tiptoed to the window. The large greenish-white moon, as if released from her moorings, had swung free of the clouds and now shone down upon snow-covered hills. Forests of spruce and cottonwood lay densely black in the valleys. A few trees, like the remnants of a scattered army, marched in single file up the steep sides of Denny's Mountain. Zack's binoculars followed them to the very top but he was unable to see the outline of his former cabin. Gray-white . . . gray-white everywhere. Now to the left, now to the right moved the binoculars. Then suddenly they hit upon a pinpoint of yellow and Zack gave a muffled exclamation. A light, like a firefly in a swamp mist, flickered and then disappeared.

Could it have been his imagination? Zack pressed closer to the window. There it was again . . . that same pinpoint of yellow! Then, unexpectedly, it flashed a steady stream of golden light.

"There they are!" and Zack, pleased that his trick had worked, gave a faint chuckle. "I'll bet Mat's feet were cold and he wouldn't turn in without a fire. And Joe's mad. They're hunting for firewood . . . just like I used to. So they're following . . . ready to grab the boy the minute I leave him. . . ."

For a long time he stood there, a thoughtful scowl upon his face. Downstairs all was still. Now and then could be heard the snap of burning wood, the dull thud of a log as it settled in its bed of ashes. The sharp creak of house timber, expanding with spring thaw, finally roused him. Moving carefully, he returned to his pack, replaced the binoculars and brought out his police diary. With the aid of a small flashlight, he made a few notes and was about to slip the book into his bag once more when his eyes caught the faint outline of something on his pillow. A note! Instinctively he knew it was from Kop-a. The writing was penciled in a firm upright hand and read:

Dear Zack—

If it's all right with you, I'd like to go north with you in the morning. Please wake me up when you read this so we can talk it over. I can pay my own way and will try to help all I can. Be sure and wake me.

K.

Zack read the note carefully for the second time and then looked across at the sleeping boy. Evidently he had crawled into his bag fully dressed, prepared to leave at a moment's notice. Only a sweater hung among the hooks on the wall at the foot of his bunk. But the memory of Kop-a's weariness, as he sat beside the fire downstairs only a few hours ago, decided Zack.

"No, youngster, I'm not waking you to-night. You need all the sleep you can get."

It had taken tact and almost force to make Kop-a come with him as far as Henry's roadhouse. Now the boy wanted to travel with him! What had caused this change? Certainly Kop-a had been stirred by the mention of Lucas' name during dinner. Was the boy connected in some way with the reindeer problem? Was he a friend or foe of Lucas? It was plain that he heartily despised Mat and Joe. Had he decided to run the risk of being sent back to the States by the Mounted Police rather than be captured by Mat and Joe and lose the puppy as well? Pondering, Zack sat on the edge of his bunk. The moon, riding high, bathed the floor at his feet in a white shaft of light from the single window. And all the while, the bright eyes of the puppy in the opposite bunk were watching.

Early in the morning, Zack was awakened by peculiar scratching sounds. Then something fell and there were muffled cries. Soon he heard the opening of a door and E. B.'s voice accompanied by protesting squeals which were undoubtedly Soapy Smith's.

"You little limb of Satan! If I ever catch you doing that again!"

There was a grunt, the sound of clawed feet scrambling over the snow crust outside, and the door shut again. Zack looked across at Kop-a's bunk. He had not stirred in his sleep throughout the night, although the puppy had moved out of sight and was probably sound asleep further down in the bag. Moving cautiously, Zack dressed and quietly made his way down the stairs. It was important that he talk with Mrs. Henry before Kop-a came down.

Mrs. Henry was setting the table at the farther end of the long room which was still quite dark and dimly lighted by a kerosene lamp. She looked up as he entered.

"Have a good night's rest?" she inquired.

"Wonderful," replied Zack. "It seemed like old times to open my eyes and see those familiar knotholes overhead."

"I was afraid E. B. would wake you up before it was time. He discovered a leg dangling in the fireplace and found Soapy stuck in the chimney. He was probably after honey in the storeroom. And when he finally came through . . . you never saw such a dirty little animal in all your life! Is Kop-a awake?"

"Not yet. I wanted to talk with you before he came down. Did you find out anything?"

"Not as much as I'd like. But it may help a little and I'll talk fast and tell each thing as it happened. I showed him around upstairs last night. He's interested in bearskins and asked to see the one in my room. Said you told him about it and he hopes to kill a bear himself some day. Well, I pointed it out and he admired it very much.

"When he noticed the poem about the snowbird which hangs on my wall by the door, he walked right over to it and stood there, reading it to himself word for word as if he knew and loved every line of it. And while I watched him, it dawned on me that the Eskimo word for snowbird is 'kop-a-noo,' and you had told me he spelt his name K-o-p-a. So I said, 'Kop-a-noo, that's a bit like your name, isn't it?' and he answered, 'It *is* my name.' I guess I must have looked surprised. 'But you aren't an Eskimo boy,' I told him and he said, 'Oh, no, but I've been called Kop-a for a long while. The kop-a-noos generally arrive at the coast on my birthday.'

"Then he spied those fawnskins which the young herder left here and which I'm making into shirts and socks for E. B. He looked them over very carefully and made the remark that the fawns had died very young. By that time, I guess he thought he had said too much, because he became very polite and there was a queer expression in his eyes as though perhaps he'd said too much and didn't intend to become too friendly with me. Later, I heard him coughing . . ."

"Yes, I saw the cup. It looked familiar."

"Hot malted milk, just as I used to fix it for you. He drank it, and then I discovered that he had a little puppy in the bag with him. Isn't that just like a boy! He must have slipped downstairs and out into the barn after it while I was in the kitchen. Now Zack, this is what I think is important. You heard him drop that spoon last night when Lucas' name was mentioned, didn't you?"

"Yes, I noticed."

"I knew you did. He knows Lucas. I'm sure of it. So then I purposely described that scene of reindeer in the ice corrals to see how he would react. Did you happen to see his face while I was talking?"

"No. He sat facing you."

"Yes, I could look directly at him. Well, when I got

as far as painting the sunset, he sat forward in his chair . . . there was almost a smile on his face and his eyes fairly shone. It was as if to say, 'I know what you are describing . . . I've seen it . . . I've been there! It will make a great picture . . .' And then he remembered where he was and drew back into the shadows. Zack, I love that boy. For a few moments he was himself, happy, enthusiastic and the way he should be. He's connected in some way with people down north and has seen reindeer. And he's been lonesome . . . homesick, eating his heart out. That name 'Kop-a' is just a term of endearment, a nickname; he's got a good American name which he's trying to hide. He's thin because he hasn't eaten properly for a long time . . . probably too unhappy where he was. What do you think, Zack, have I hit it anywhere near right?"

"Sounds reasonable. What you say is all very possible," and Zack scowled thoughtfully. "You've been a big help, Mrs. Henry. It's a lead and I'll keep checking on it."

"From what he said, I think he's planning to go along with you this morning."

"Yes, he left a note on my pillow."

"Oh, Zack! Do you think it's best?" There was sharp concern in Mrs. Henry's voice. She had finished setting the table and now came around to where Zack stood. "Why, E. B. says you're going through the Lost Lands. That will be a hard trip for a boy. It's bad enough to have you go! Those lakes . . . there are so many of them, and you'll have to cross Ivory Horn. It would take weeks to go round it. And those squalls . . . they're merciless!"

"I know," agreed Zack. "On the other hand, if I leave him here, somebody will pick him up. He's safer with me. Had you thought of that? Nobody can take him from me because I represent the law. And I shan't turn him loose until I see where he's headed for and what it's all about. I'll take good care of him."

"Of course. I know you will," and Mrs. Henry sighed and shook her head. "E. B. and I would love to have a boy like him around here. If he's just drifting, Zack, bring him back. And if you insist on taking him, do wait over a day or so. You both need a rest. I've tried and tried to think where I have seen those dark eyes and light hair before." Mrs. Henry sighed again. "You'd think I'd remember every living soul who ever came through here but I don't. It's surprising how many strangers stop here. And of course it's three years since I went Outside to the States. This boy is part of a hazy picture. If only I could place him . . . maybe I shall before you leave. What about supplies? You'll need extra if he goes along. And you'll wait over a day or so?"

"I will. You're right, as usual. It may give him a better break and meanwhile we can keep the radio tuned to the Signals Station at Aklavik. We may hear something. There's a list somewhere," and Zack fished about in his pockets. He finally produced a slip of paper and handed it to Mrs. Henry.

"Five pounds of lard, five pounds of hardtack, two pounds of chocolate, dehydrated potatoes, cheese, six cans of beans, sugar, flour and all the powdered milk you can spare," she read slowly. "I suppose that milk's for the boy. I'll add some prunes and dried apples, too. E. B.'s filling the oil drums right now and Raven will have some cooked dog food ready for you. And while I think of it, E. B. has an ice chisel which he wants to give you. It has a long handle and can be used to measure the depth of the ice after you have cut through. It's something new. You know how that lake ice candles in the spring. I wish I were going with you . . ."

Mrs. Henry's sentence remained unfinished. Footsteps were heard on the stairs and Kop-a appeared with the puppy under one arm. A look of relief flashed across his face as his searching eyes spied Zack.

"Feel all right this morning, son?" called Mrs. Henry.

Kop-a returned her smile and nodded. "Fine, thank you," but his eyes again sought Zack anxiously. "Did you get my note?" he asked.

"Yes, I have it." Zack patted his pocket. "But I hated to wake you and thought we might just as well talk this morning. You don't think you can wait for Jon Mitchen?"

"No." Kop-a shook his head decidedly.

"I wonder if you know what you're in for, traveling with the police. We don't travel like the regular musher."

"I know," and Kop-a looked back at him frankly. "Anyway, I don't want to travel with anyone else. I've got some money . . ." There was a pleading note in his voice.

"The money isn't the important part," replied Zack.

"It's the uncertainty of everything. I might not get as far as the coast. I might strike a fresh clue and have to double back on my tracks. Worse yet, I'm going into a country filled with lakes. I hope to go across Ivory Horn, as it would take days to go around it and the river at the head of the lake has a strong current. But I mean to reach the coast as soon as I can, according to present plans. You'll be taking quite a few risks traveling with me."

"But I'm willing to take the risks," said Kop-a. There was a persistent quality in his voice and his eyes were direct and earnest.

"Well, I've warned you," said Zack. "In case I did let you come and anything happened to you, is there anyone who should be notified?"

"No one." Kop-a shook his head. "No one," he repeated.

Mrs. Henry opened her mouth as if to speak but with an effort refrained from doing so. Her manner suggested that she intended to leave the matter wholly in Zack's hands. But as she looked again at the thin boy before her, clutching his still thinner puppy, the words came out in spite of herself.

"Zack, if you take him, I'll add some malted milk to your order. Drink it hot every night and give the puppy some, too."

"Good idea," said Zack.

"Then I'm going with you?" Kop-a asked eagerly.

"Well, I guess you are," said Zack slowly. "As a matter of fact, I decided last night that it would be all right, but it was only fair to let you know in advance what you're in for. If I have to turn back before we reach the coast, it will be your hard luck. And here's a little surprise for you. We aren't starting today, which is just as well for you. We'll leave tomorrow morning instead."

"That's fine." There was a flash of happiness and relief in Kop-a's eyes, and it actually seemed to Zack as if the puppy's worried expression disappeared as well.

Raven, passing by with a large pot of coffee, stopped. "That dog different," he commented.

"What do you mean, Raven; why is he different?" asked Mrs. Henry.

Raven shook his head as though he himself were puzzled. "He different," the Eskimo insisted. "He have big nose. Puppee smell many things." He held the steaming coffee a little closer.

The fragrance of the coffee seemed to be of vital interest to the small dog. His head was back, his black nose sniffing the air, his round eyes questioning.

"You see?" asked Raven.

"Raven knows dogs pretty well and I'd take his word for it," said Zack. "The pup did follow that trail in good shape yesterday. He looks like a little roughneck right now, but maybe he has good blood in him, Kop-a."

"Cereal's ready," called Mrs. Henry. "Raven, tell E. B. And bring the puppy over here, Kop-a. A little cereal won't hurt him either."

The sun was well over the horizon when Zack and Kop-a were ready to start on the second morning.

Raven and E. B. had stored the packs and food on the sled while Zack fastened down the tarpaulin.

"You have no letters or messages to leave with me?" Mrs. Henry asked Zack.

With her hood thrown back and her cheeks glowing with the morning air, Mrs. Henry looked as though she might have joined them if she had had the slightest excuse. Her eyes searched the white land ahead as a sailor gazes longingly over the sea. Soapy Smith, a small black spot on the landscape, sat at some distance, still conscious of his disgrace and not daring to come near.

"No letters," replied Zack. "I'm alone now since my uncle died. If I shouldn't come back," and Zack hesitated a bit awkwardly, "I left some things in a safe at Regina. They've got your names on them . . ."

"You'll be coming back," interrupted E. B. gruffly. "You'll probably be a sergeant the next time we see you. Now don't forget, if you get separated on the tundra, don't waste your time traveling around in circles. It's hopeless. Aim north and you'll meet on the coast. More than one man has gone bush crazy in the Lost Lands. Is this the same lead dog you had last year, Zack? The one who likes to hunt?"

"The same one," said Zack. "He's got the whole pack trained now to help him. They're not afraid to tackle anything. Barry over there is one of Susie's litter. This is his first trip. Wants to play, and grins all the time like a big fat baby."

"He'll be a good dog when he grows up. Did you

fasten the ice chisel on, Raven?" E. B.'s keen eyes were noting every detail of Zack's equipment.

"I fix it," answered Raven.

"I guess you're all set then," and E. B.'s pleasant face seemed unusually sober. "I wish you'd tell us a little more about what you're doing and where you're going, but if you can't, why, you can't. 'The Silent Force' . . . that's a good name for your organization. But remember what I told you last night and keep your wits about you. We'll be looking for you on the way back."

"I'll be here."

"Good-bye, Zack." Mrs. Henry put both hands on the young corporal's shoulders and her eyes were unnaturally bright. "Godspeed all the way and back again."

They all watched silently as Kop-a slipped beneath the bear robe on the sled with the puppy beside him.

"We see you some day?" Raven had taken quite a fancy to the boy.

"Of course," and Kop-a nodded his head quickly. Almost submerged under the bearskin, he looked up at them, a slight lonely figure and strangely apart. On a sudden impulse, Mrs. Henry leaned over the sled and kissed him.

"Good-bye, Kop-a-noo," she whispered.

"Good-bye," he answered. There was an eager response in his voice and as the sled pulled away, the bell ringing, she caught a grateful flash from his dark eyes.

CHAPTER SEVEN

Starting Northward

WHEN Zack started northward, he was traveling over unfamiliar territory. The country north of his old patrol consisted of mountains, lakes, rivers, and vast stretches of tundra seldom crossed by man, and was known as the Lost Lands. With only maps and compass to guide him, this hazardous trek would require all his courage and skill. But a slight sense of foreboding seized him as the last well-known landmark disappeared. For the first time he began to question his own judgment in allowing Kop-a to accompany him. His final decision had been swayed by some inner hunch and now that cold reason had begun to assert itself, Zack was uneasy.

Kop-a was alert and intelligent, but would he be able to fulfill his quota of work upon such a trip? Reticent and aloof, he had conducted himself at the Henrys' roadhouse with an astuteness beyond his years. But upon becoming better acquainted, would he talk too much, ask needless questions and finally lapse into the role of an indolent passenger? And what of his relationship with Lucas? Was he friend or enemy?

As to the name Kop-a-noo, it was perhaps an affectionate term, as Mrs. Henry shrewdly surmised, bestowed upon him by natives. Had not Amundsen been called "King-Ok-puk," meaning "Big Nose," and Stefansson "Neokok Too-tee-lakh" or "The-Man-Who-Measures-Heads?" Would not a small white boy whose birthday came the day the kop-a-noos arrived in the spring very likely be called "Snow Bird?" And later, wishing to conceal his identity, would he not naturally use this name in an emergency?

All these questions Zack asked himself as he drove his dogs forward on the first lap of his journey into the unknown. Though he had listened to the radio station at Aklavik the day before, he had heard nothing that could be connected with Kop-a. News of illegal hunting of musk oxen in the Thelon Game Sanctuary had come over the wire, also word that the *Macdonald*, R.M.P. cruiser, had rescued a disabled fishing boat off the Atlantic coast . . . but there was no announcement of a runaway boy. Whoever was searching for Kop-a was working quietly.

To be sure, before leaving Henrys' that morning, there had been a pathetic eagerness in the way Kop-a had tried to assist in the loading of the sled. There was something almost feverish in his effort to be of use, carrying the heavy dunnage bags down the stairs and untangling the knots of ropes which held the tarpaulin down. It was as though he were fearful of being left behind at the very last moment. Improved by his day's rest, he coughed less frequently, choking each occasional attack in his throat or stifling it in a red cashmere scarf, apparently new, which he wore about his neck. Zack had not seen the scarf before. At the very first opportunity, he determined to examine it. Possibly there would be a tradesman's label on it somewhere . . .

There was little conversation on the trail that morning. Once they stopped while Zack removed the sled bell. Kop-a watched curiously but asked no questions. For the most part, the puppy slept, though from where he stood at the handle bar, Zack saw now and then a white ear protruding from the heavy bearskin and two anxious bright eyes studying him discreetly. In the small sharp face, the eyes seemed to be abnormally large and to have a mature expression of wisdom, caution and suffering. Perhaps as the emaciated body filled out with extra feeding, the eyes would not appear so large. And he would learn to play. Barry, good-natured, clumsy Barry, the largest dog on the team but a puppy at heart, was inclined to play when Susie was not watching. Barry alone seemed friendly to the small stranger.

Geese, in wedge-shaped formation, passed overhead, flying with regular wing beats toward the coast. But it was no time to fire a rifle. The report would travel far over those unbroken spaces and their position could be located too easily. Nor were they in immediate need of food. Zack comforted himself that there would be other flocks of birds as they neared the sea.

Spring! Spring in the Arctic! In Regina, maple buds hung in red lacy sprays above the quiet dirt roads, but here . . . Zack looked about him curiously. Ahead and on both sides of him stretched plains of flawless white. Here and there, one might peer into a shallow valley lined with stunted evergreens, shrubs struggling to maintain life in a rocky soil scarcely thawed in the short summer months. And later, he had been told, one might pass through almost impassible thickets of tall and healthy willows, ready to burst into bluish-green leaves. A strange and eerie world this . . . with the sun swinging in a great circle, hanging over the horizon directly south at noon and traveling to the north, just out of sight below the sky line, for its midnight hour.

Zack was suddenly aroused from his thoughts by a sharp gust of wind which tore at him from the northeast. Clouds had gathered gray and heavy overhead, and for the past few minutes he had been vaguely conscious that the dogs were lagging. Moise, his white head turned over his shoulder, had been trying to tell him that a storm was ahead.

"All right, old fellow, we'll stop soon," called Zack, and Moise quieted.

"There's a storm coming," Zack explained to Kop-a. "From now on I'll stop and cut spruce for beds as we go along. Do you remember where E. B. packed that small hatchet?"

"It's between the grub box and the small bag," answered Kop-a immediately. Zack nodded his appreciation. If Kop-a continued to be observing, he would be useful.

"Here, you hold the dogs while I cut," and he gave the reins to the boy. With the small hatchet, he carefully removed a single green branch from a nearby spruce and then passed on to another low-growing tree a few feet distant. This procedure continued until there was a sufficient supply, Kop-a watching curiously and the puppy's head again peering over his shoulder with a similar expression.

"All set," announced Zack, giving a swift look at the

sky. "We've just about time enough to stake the dogs, feed them, and put up the tent. We'll steer over to that level place by the rock. I keep away from deep hollows during storms. The snow piles up and it's hard work to dig out."

Kop-a nodded and passed him the reins.

"You could feed the dogs," Zack continued. "Do you know where the fish is packed?"

"Yes."

"Good. That's your job then. Give each dog three fish. One for the pup. We mustn't overfeed him."

Zack, having staked the dogs, turned his attention to cutting blocks of snow with a small handsaw. These he arranged in a circle as a windbreak and stretched over them a tent of canvas, weighing the outer edges down with more blocks of snow. He worked quickly, gazing up at the sky frequently, and had just finished when he caught sight of Kop-a nearby. The dogs had been fed.

"Ever see a tent fixed like this?"

"No." Kop-a shook his head.

"How long does it take to build a *too-boo-ga-roo?*" asked Zack quickly.

"Not long if the sod has been cut."

So Kop-a was familiar with the *too-boo-ga-roos*, the mound-shaped huts made of willows bent at the top, tied, covered with sod, and commonly used by herders on the range. Then Mrs. Henry had been correct. The boy was familiar with the reindeer country. The question, quickly put, had brought forth an immediate answer.

"I understand there are only a few Eskimos living

who build an igloo well," Zack continued casually. There was no answer and Zack knew that Kop-a was now on guard. "Want to pile that spruce inside while I unpack? Put it together at the far end to give us as much room as possible."

Zack stopped as he passed the dogs. "Well, knock me down, what do you know about that?" Susie held the squirming puppy with a firm forepaw while she washed his face. Barry, staked close by, stood at pleased attention, as if relieved that another face was now to be washed.

"Guess Ruff is making friends," said a voice at Zack's elbow. Kop-a was watching also.

"Ruff? Is that what you call him?"

"Yes. You called him a roughneck back at Henry's and I thought it was a good name for him. Ruff, for short."

Almost as soon as the sled had been unloaded and the necessary contents carried into the tent, the storm broke. The dogs, in preparedness, curled themselves into balls, their noses hidden beneath their bushy tails. It was as if winter, working northward, were keeping pace with them. A wind, with a shrill decisive shriek, brought snow from the west in slithering sheets across the tundra. Little eddies of snow whirled in the more sheltered places. A curtain of white had fallen and swiftly covered the dogs who lay still to allow the snow to form a warm and protective crust over their bodies. For the moment, the puppy seemed to be content with Susie.

Outside the tent, Zack beat the two parkas free of hoarfrost and tossed them just inside the tent where they would not thaw and become damp. A kettle of snow was put on the Primus stove to melt. The young corporal moved about his duties with an ease born of practice.

"Think we'll have some of Mrs. Henry's ham and eggs for supper and top it off with apple pie," he announced. "She fixed us up a nice box . . . put some jam in, too."

"Sounds good," said Kop-a, and Zack smiled at the genuine enthusiasm in the boy's voice.

So far, Kop-a had proved companionable. There had been no needless questions asked all that day and no complaints of weariness or cold.

"What'd I do with that knife, drat it! Here it is," and Zack kept up an easy run of conversation. "Later we'll unroll those skins and sleeping bags and place them on the spruce boughs. Just as good as a hair mattress."

"I've been wondering," Kop-a hesitated a bit, "why you cut one branch at a time so carefully from each tree. I suppose there's a reason."

"Yes, there is a reason," replied Zack. "Anyone following our trail would spot a tree entirely stripped of its branches. But a branch gone here or there would never be noticed. An old Indian taught me that. Simple but safe."

"I understand now," said the boy slowly. "You think we're being followed. That's why you took off the sled bell."

"I'm not sure we're being followed. I do know, as I told you before, there were lights on Denny's Mountain two nights ago. Whether Mat and Joe are right behind us or taking the mountain route is the question. The mountain route is a short cut to Ivory Horn Lake but it's tough going. It's hard on the dogs. And camping on the side of a windy precipice is no joke. I lost a tent that way once. If Mat is on the precipice to-night in this storm, you can just bet his feet are plenty cold."

The water was boiling now and Zack moved the pan aside to make room for the skillet in which he laid a slice of ham. But it was evident that Kop-a had another question to ask. He moved about restlessly and twice drew in his breath sharply as if he were about to speak.

"Anything more?" asked Zack.

"Yes, if you don't mind. If the Michauds asked you to turn me over to them, would you have to do it?"

"Not by a long shot," answered Zack with emphasis. "I'd place you under arrest myself. You'd be my prisoner."

"That's what I thought," nodded Kop-a. He appeared slightly relieved and seemed to be gathering courage to ask another question. It came suddenly, the boy's dark eyes gazing directly at Zack.

"Am I your prisoner now?"

"Lord, no," and Zack gave a faint chuckle. "You asked to come, didn't you?"

"Yes, I did. I had my reasons . . . my reasons for asking. Have you any idea Mat and Joe will follow us all the way to the coast?"

"No idea." Zack turned the ham over and there was a loud sizzling noise. "It all depends," he continued after a few moments, "on what information Mat and Joe got from Ole. If there's a big reward offered for you, they'll probably follow. The Michauds are greedy. There was no radio announcement about you yesterday. And it may be that the Michauds have business in the very direction we are going. It wouldn't surprise me if they were trying to tip someone off that I'm coming. Your guess to-night is just as good as mine. Hello, pup! You're such a privileged character around here, I suppose you're going to join us for supper."

Ruff's black nose, sniffing at the tent flap, was all there was to be seen. But at the cordial note in Zack's voice, he immediately squeezed himself through an unbelievably small space and entered, his black coat wet and his tiny plumed tail wagging.

"There's a leash in the bag, Kop-a. And tie the end to something or he'll be in the ham. He'd eat us out of house and home if we'd let him. He's just finished one supper."

The leash did not seem to bother Ruff particularly as he was interested in the cooking operations. He seated himself by Kop-a, his eyes bulging brightly, his mouth open. The tent was filled with fumes of the frying meat.

"He's looking better already, isn't he?" said Kop-a, laying a possessive hand on the puppy's back. "Raven said he'd like to have him. But somehow, I didn't want to leave him behind. Seemed like double-crossing."

Zack looked up quickly. Kop-a looked fairly happy as he sat there, his cap pushed back, showing his light hair, the red scarf hanging loosely about his neck, and one hand smoothing the dog at his side. The roar of the storm had not dampened his spirits and he was as interested as the puppy in the cooking of the ham. Somewhere, someone was worrying about him. Refined, well mannered, he was hardly the type to have spent much time in the extreme north. And yet he had seen *too-boo-ga-roos* and knew how they were built. This meant he had come from the coast when old enough to take a keen interest in his surroundings. Possibly last year or the year before . . . Zack, almost lost in his reflections, came back to their conversation with an effort.

"I know what you mean. Dogs in the north are almost like people. I had to leave Lingo behind on the trail once. She was sick and I had a heavy load. There was just a chance that she might pull through by herself so I left her, rather than shoot her. She was too weak to walk but she sat up and stared after me as I drove away. I didn't sleep much that night. Her eyes haunted me, and before dawn I decided to dress and go back for her. But when I went outside to harness up, there she was, curled up with the other dogs. From then on, I cached some of the load and carried her on the sled until she was well."

"Moise is different from your other dogs," observed Kop-a.

"Yes, he's a one-man dog. He's no mixer. That's his nature. Ruff here is something like him. Your puppy would make a good tracker."

"A tracker?"

"Yes, a dog to follow trails. At Rockcliffe Kennels, the Force trains dogs to do all sorts of work. It takes about eighty lessons to train one dog. Have you ever heard of our dogs Dale, Black Lux, Sultan, or Tell?"

"No." Kop-a was interested. "I'd like to hear about them sometime. Do you think Ruff could be taught to trail?"

"Wouldn't be surprised. We might try him out some day."

"That would be great." The boy's face was alight with enthusiasm and his voice friendly. "A fellow learns a lot at Regina, doesn't he? I suppose you had a stiff course in rifle practice, didn't you?"

"I'll say."

"I'd rather shoot a gun than do anything else in the world! Sol, a friend of mine, used to let me practice on his. Sol was a good shot and he said it wouldn't take me long to learn. I tried to buy one in Nor . . ." Here Kop-a stammered and flushed a bit. "In a place south of here," he finished lamely, "but they wouldn't sell to a minor."

"No, they have to be very strict."

"I know a fellow whose uncle belonged to the Force," continued Kop-a. "He must have been a good shot because he won the gold crossed-rifle badge. I suppose you've seen it . . . it's quite an honor to win it."

"Yes, I've seen it," replied Zack.

"Did you try for it?" persisted Kop-a.

"Yes. . . . The ham's done. Hold your plate over here, but first shorten that leash or you'll have Ruff in your plate. Don't burn yourself. I'll fry the eggs in a minute."

Ruff was fastened closer to the tent pole, but Kop-a's mind was not on what he was doing. As he held his plate out for the ham, his eyes searched Zack's face carefully. There was a growing light of comprehension in them and he seemed to come to some decision.

"Some day," and he spoke quietly, "I hope you'll show me the rifle badge you won. I've never seen one."

Zack, surprised, looked up quickly. This boy was no fool.

CHAPTER EIGHT

A Letter From Lucas

BEFORE he answered, Zack broke two eggs into the skillet, his mind working rapidly. Finally he looked up at the boy and smiled.

"I guess Raven's been talking to you. You spent quite a lot of time with him yesterday."

"Yes, he showed me around. All he said, though, was that you were one of the best shots on the Force. I put two and two together. Do you have the badge with you?"

"No, I left it with some things in Regina. How does that dinner taste?"

"Fine." Kop-a ate hungrily. "I'd like to live this way all the time." He gazed about him eagerly. "The farther we get away from houses and streets, the better I like it. All that smoke and noise is like a bad dream." He motioned with one hand towards the south. "I hope I never have to go back there again. Why is it a fellow learns to love the north so much?"

"I guess it's because it's so clean and quiet and it's . . ." Zack searched for a word . . . "it's timeless. This country around here will look just the same next year. A man can't make a dent in it. And ten years from now, it will probably be like this. There aren't any frills down here. A man's on his own. One fellow may speak a little better English but he's got to eat the same food and wear the same skins as his neighbor. The north is a leveler. I like it." Zack nodded his head contentedly. "I don't mind being alone. You can think down here. And I've seen some beautiful sights."

"What?" asked Kop-a.

"Oh, just little things. Nothing you'd notice maybe. But after a while they seem to sink into you and then you're looking for them. I've come out of my tent in the morning and found frost flowers all over the place."

"I've seen them," injected the boy quickly.

"Sometimes at noon a whole valley of pine glistens as if it were hung with diamonds. And at night there's nothing prettier than blue and purple shadows on the snow." This was a somewhat flowery speech for Zack to make, and he halted as though conscious of it. "You learn to see little things in the north. Things you haven't time for in the big cities."

"I know," answered Kop-a. "Sometimes last winter I tried to imagine I was here and there weren't any houses and streets. That I had on snowshoes and could see nothing but snow . . ."

"The north has lured many a person from home." Zack paused and stared fully half a minute at Kop-a before he spoke again. "But if I thought someone was worrying about my being here, I couldn't enjoy it. If I thought my father or mother . . ."

"There's no one worrying about me, if that's what you mean," replied the boy, instantly on the defensive. "The people who are looking for me are worrying about the money they might lose if they don't find me. All they care about is money. They wouldn't really care what happened to me. And the people . . . or the person who ought to care something about me . . . well, they're thinking of other things."

Zack remained silent. Perhaps now, Kop-a was about to confide in him.

"You love your work and that's all you think of," continued the boy after a pause. "The law means everything to you. If it tells you to do a certain thing, you do it, whether it breaks a person's heart or not. I'd like to talk to you, but I can't. An hour from now if your friend Sergeant Cunningham showed up, you might turn me right over to him, saying you had decided it was your duty. I don't trust the law. It has no feelings."

"But the law does have feelings," remonstrated Zack. "Why, if I were the cold-blooded machine you think I am, I'd have left you with the Henrys. You'd be traveling south with the Michauds by now. To hear you talk anyone would think the Force was a bunch of head-hunters. Like most boys, I suppose you think our slogan is 'Get Your Man!' "

"Isn't it?"

"No!" Zack put down his knife and fork, scorn in his face. "If there's anything that disgusts me, it's to hear those three words, 'Get Your Man!' They have nothing to do with the Force! Some cheap dime novel writer must have started it, and now we hear it from all parts of the globe. I heard the Commissioner himself say once that he was looking for the man who first said it. '*Maintiens le Droit*' is our motto. It means to uphold the law and all that is good and fair and right. Justice! Men have fought and bled and died for that motto. Of course we have to go out and accomplish what we're sent to do. If we didn't, what kind of an organization would we have? If we arrest a criminal, he's brought back in good condition or we have to explain why. He is kept warm, fed and looked after, many times when the member of the Force in charge is deprived."

Zack's voice became more gentle. "You've been listening to hearsay. You'd be surprised to know of the different kinds of work we have to do. Life in the wilderness demands strange things. Many a young constable has had to set bones, deliver babies, and nurse mothers. Many an officer has swept a kitchen floor and been sent out, the next instant, on a mission of utmost importance and secrecy. The law does have feelings," Zack repeated earnestly. "It isn't hard, cruel, merciless. Why, I've wanted to help you. I thought you had a lot of grit coming down here alone and trying to make your way to the coast. Not every boy would tackle it. You know Lucas Joules, don't you?" asked Zack suddenly.

"Yes, I know Lucas," breathed Kop-a. He was staring wide-eyed at the young corporal, his hands clenched. The red scarf had fallen from his shoulders.

"I was pretty sure you did," said Zack.

"Well, what about it?" asked the boy, suppressed anger and distrust in his voice.

"You're not sure but you think perhaps I'm after Lucas. That's why you decided to stick along with me. I might get to the coast sooner than you and you want me where you can keep an eye on me, even at the expense of running into danger yourself. I like your courage."

"Thanks." Kop-a sat erect and tense.

"We both know Lucas. It's too bad we can't get together and discuss what we know and see if we can help him . . ."

"Help him? How do I know you're his friend?" The boy reminded Zack of a young animal, guarded, ready to strike back. "You say he saved your life but if the law sent you to arrest him, you'd have to do it, wouldn't you? You're a corporal. How do I know but what you've been promised a promotion if you arrest Lucas? Maybe you'll be made a sergeant if you can bring him in."

"If Lucas has broken the law, I'll bring him in. As a matter of fact, I'm going to the coast to help him."

Kop-a remained silent, unconvinced, his dark eyes wary.

"You'll have to take my word for it, son. And my word means something, as I said before. You're a white boy and Lucas is an Eskimo. Why should you be so concerned over Lucas' affairs?"

Outside a gust of sleet slashed against the sides of the tent and nearly lifted it bodily from its foundations. Ruff crouched in sudden fright, pulling at the leash in a vain effort to reach the boy who seemed unconscious of his surroundings. The wind screamed across the tundra to the east and in the lull which followed, Kop-a's words sounded with a singular clearness.

"I'll tell you why I'm concerned over Lucas. Lucas

is my friend . . . my friend, do you understand? And if I thought you were going to the coast to arrest him for something he never did," and he leaned closer, his eyes smoldering, "I'd do anything to stop you. Anything. I'd see that you never got there. That's what Lucas means to me."

Zack carefully studied the boy before him. Here was courage, loyalty. Whatever the effort, Kop-a was worth seeing through. Shy, lonely, he probably had few friends. Those few he loved ardently. And he hated as he loved . . . a nature of extremes.

In the silence which followed, Ruff whimpered and Kop-a unconsciously put out a hand and patted the still crouching puppy. There was a wan, unhappy expression on his face as though already he regretted his outburst of temper.

"I guess I'm beginning to understand you," said Zack. "You hate and you love hard."

The boy nodded silently but it was some time before he spoke. "Lucas was awfully good to me when I was a kid. I like Eskimos."

"I see." Zack, touched by this acknowledgment, leaned forward and opened his personal dunnage bag. From a folder, he drew a letter.

"I can't read all of this letter to you, because some of it is confidential. But I can read a part. You know Lucas' handwriting, don't you?" and he held out the envelope to the boy.

In the dim light, Kop-a stared closely at the fine slanting handwriting and then nodded his head. "It's Lucas' all right."

The letter was long and filled with fine script. Zack turned the pages until he came to the last paragraph. "Here, read this with me," he offered. He pushed the letter nearer and read aloud, with Kop-a following the lines.

"In-a-loo sends her love and says it will be a glad day when you come. She has some eider duck eggs stored away for you in the frozen rocks back of our house. She still remembers how much you liked them at Harris Bay."

"Harris Bay!" exclaimed Kop-a. "Why, that's where Lucas and In-a-loo go to visit their cousins in Alaska!" There was glad recognition in his voice as if he had not heard the words for a long time.

"That's where I first met them," answered Zack. "Lucas had some fox skins to trade in and In-a-loo was excited over buying cotton for dresses. They spoke good English and told me they had been educated at a Mission school on the coast. Lucas had been to Seattle. After that I saw quite a bit of Lucas. He took me walrus hunting. Later he came to my rescue when I was drifting on an ice floe. I've never seen where they lived."

"It's a house built out of the hull of a schooner," Kop-a informed him eagerly. "I can just remember when it washed ashore in the spring breakup. Lucas made a nice house out of it. I used to like to go down there. He'd do the Iyak-hok with a piece of string and carve ivory figures for me."

"The Iyak-hok, that's something like the cat's cradle, isn't it?"

"Something like it but a lot harder to do . . . Once when I was sick I kept yelling for Lucas. Finally he and In-a-loo bundled me up and took me to their home. Then I got well."

Kop-a's face was lighted with happy memories as he talked. He was finding it a relief to be able to speak freely. Suddenly a shadow seemed to blot out the light and he looked across at Zack with concern in his eyes.

"How do they say Lucas caught the deer? Is he supposed to have shot them?"

"No, a rawhide noose, sixty feet long, was used. The herders found its tracks in the snow."

"Lucas wouldn't do a thing like that," declared Kop-a indignantly. "His ancestors were chiefs and fine people. He's proud of them and proud of the labret he inherited. It's worth a good deal of money. An art collector tried to buy it but Lucas wouldn't sell. I've seen it . . . it's like a big green button. Lucas' grandfather used to wear it in a slit in his lower lip."

"There are still a few old men around wearing them."

"Yes, I've seen them," answered the boy.

Kop-a was himself now, but made no further effort to talk. He finished his supper in an abstracted manner, giving the last piece of ham on his plate to Ruff, who swallowed it in one gulp. The red scarf had slipped further down his back and now hung over one of the rear guy ropes.

After they had finished their tea, the boy opened the conversation again. "I guess I was pretty quick on the trigger back there. But the idea of anyone taking

Lucas to jail just makes me see red. How long do you think it will take us to reach the coast?" There was suppressed excitement in his voice and his hands moved restlessly. "I'm in a hurry to get there."

"I wish I knew," answered Zack. "A lot depends on the weather. Storms like this don't help."

"Raven says that not many people travel this route. It's tough going. I suppose you have a good reason for going this way."

"There's always a reason," answered Zack with a smile, "why a policeman does the unusual. But I can tell you this . . . I don't believe I'll be taking Lucas to jail. I am jailing the man who stole Paul Buckley's deer. Of course you must remember that the white man's ways spoil some of the Eskimos. Money comes easy and they get soft."

"Not Lucas," said Kop-a stoutly. "He won't change. Neither will Sol. Did you happen to see Sol Goodhope at Harris Bay?"

"No, there was no Sol Goodhope at Harris Bay."

"He's Lucas' cousin. He makes trips with explorers."

Kop-a had begun to run his hand over the heavy canvas bags back of him. "Do you suppose we could play your phonograph while we wash the dishes? No one could hear it, could they?"

"Not with this rain," answered Zack.

Rain was beating down steadily with a loud drumming sound against the tent. In a few moments, strains of music rose above the sound of the downpour, and continued throughout the evening. Later, as the two travelers lay in their bags, the small puppy rolled in a deerskin between them, the stars shone out of a moonlit sky on an ice-gleaming world below.

But Zack did not fall asleep immediately. After waiting for the boy's breathing to become slow and regular, and when it seemed certain that he was no longer awake, Zack reached for his flashlight. Though the puppy stirred, he did not growl as the light flitted across the face of his young master. Kop-a had fallen asleep with a faint smile on his lips, as if his last thoughts had been happy ones. The unnatural strained expression was completely erased from his countenance and he slept peacefully.

"Blamed if he isn't a swell kid," said Zack softly to himself, flitting the light back and forth gently. "Did him good to talk a little. And he knows Sol. Good old Sol! Finest guide on the coast. I still want to look at that scarf."

Moving carefully, he reached for the scarf, which by now had fallen between two dunnage bags. It took but a few moments to see that the trade tag had been removed.

CHAPTER NINE

On the Shore of Ivory Horn Lake

"STEADYING the sled," as Zack described it that next morning on the trail, was not the easiest thing in the world. Hummocks a foot high, glazed with ice, now appeared on the tundra . . . a sea of frozen ice-caps, dazzling white as far as the eye could reach. The tundra and the sky met as one, and the sled, heading northward, seemed to be embarked on an endless journey. To soften the glare of the sun on the snow, Zack and Kop-a donned amber snow glasses.

Zack, forging ahead on snowshoes, flattened the hummocks with his own weight as much as possible, while Kop-a followed, steering the sled. Up and down bobbed the sled upon its Siberian runners, the boy using all his strength at times to prevent the canvas-covered load from overturning.

Ruff ran ahead with Barry and by the appearance of his straining hindquarters, seemed to be under the illusion that he was assisting. He finally dropped back with his tongue hanging, and Kop-a, noticing his weariness, stuffed him into the bag which swung from the sled's handle bars.

Now and then a single tree appeared. Thick at the base, it grew but a few feet high with branches bent downward, warped at the sides and sprawling grotesquely umbrella-like upon the white snow. Kop-a noticed that each tree grew no higher than its shelter of rock or slight rise of hill afforded. For a continuous dry northeast wind blew across the tundra day and night, blighting any shoot of green that dared raise its head above the shelter line. This was the tundra country, of white-headed cotton grass, mosses and lichens, a reedy bog in summer where waterfowl screamed and nested.

They came to the last tree they were to pass for some time . . . a twisted misshapen mass of bark and rusty green.

"I actually feel sorry for that tree," said Zack, retracing his steps and coming back to Kop-a. "It's trying so hard to live in this northeast wind. Not much here for it . . . a few weeks of sun and a bird now and then." He stopped abruptly as his eyes rested on Kop-a. "You look sort of beat out. You'd better see how your face feels, too. If it seems numb, warm your hand inside your shirt and then reach up under the collar of your parka and rub your face. Like this . . ." As he was demonstrating, Zack suddenly asked, "Where's Ruff?"

Kop-a was warming his face with one hand and pointed at the sled bag with the other just as Ruff looked out, licking his mouth and swallowing hard.

"There goes my chocolate," said Zack.

"I'll give you some of mine," Kop-a offered hastily. "I put him in there because he was dragging behind. I didn't know you kept your chocolate in there."

"It was only an end piece. Guess we've got a Soapy

Smith with us. Before he does any more damage, pull out that roll of jerky. Want to stop for tea?"

Kop-a nodded his head quickly. He had pulled, hoisted, and balanced the sled and was breathing hard from his exertions. Zack eyed him critically. So far the boy had not complained in any way but the suggestion of rest and tea had immediately appealed to him.

"This dry air draws all the water out of your body like a sponge," said Zack. "Tea is the only drink that satisfies. I sound like an advertisement, don't I?"

The jerky rescued, Kop-a assisted Zack in cutting three blocks of snow which they placed about the primus stove as a windbreak. The snow in the kettle heated quickly and in a short time several cups of tea had warmed and rested them.

"I don't wonder E. B. said not to hunt in circles but to go straight north if we ever got lost," remarked Zack, looking about him. "But it's fine reindeer country. See all that moss over there where we dug up the blocks? That's what puts the 'back fat' on reindeer, isn't it? That and tops of willows and birch."

Suddenly Zack paused. His keen eyes had caught sight of Nigak, who was licking his fore paw. On the snow beside him were bright red stains. "What's on the snow? Blood?" Zack knelt beside the dog to examine his paw. "Well, Nigak," he said, "this crust got you plenty!"

Turning to Kop-a, he added, "This means that they've all got to wear moccasins."

Examination disclosed that Susie's feet were not hurt,

but big, awkward Barry held up one of his as though he were suffering severely. So delighted was he by the attention he was about to receive, however, that the unconcealed expression of pleasure on his face belied his pretense. Zack laughed and playfully cuffed him after examining the large black pads of his feet, which were intact.

"You big fraud! Sometimes I wonder why I let you come along."

Moise, Split and Lingo were uninjured. Zack unpacked some circular pieces of caribou skin with drawstrings of sinew, and each dog received four moccasins which were tied securely to his legs above the paws.

Meanwhile Ruff was enjoying himself. With his forefeet, he dug industriously in the shallow snow until he found a stone. Convinced that he had unearthed a valuable treasure, he ran about with it in his mouth. As he could not be persuaded to part with it, he was dropped, stone and all, into the swinging handle bag. From then on, however brief their stops, Ruff struggled to get out and add to his collection of stones. It grew rapidly and the bag began to swing with a decided momentum.

The morning passed quickly for Zack and Kop-a, despite its hard going. Although Kop-a had begun to ask questions, they were intelligent inquiries and showed a background of observation and reading. He had seen big game brought in, the hide removed and flenched, but had never been present at the actual kill.

"When I bring in a bear," he told Zack as they sat

at their brief noonday meal, "I'll feel pretty good. Sort of independent."

"Which kind are you after?" asked Zack. "Black, brown, gray or white?"

"I guess any color would do," answered the boy with a smile, "just so it's a bear. I'm going to own a gun some day," he promised himself.

As they were about to start out once more, Zack suddenly raised the rifle to his shoulder and a shot rang out. An Arctic hare stopped in its tracks, turned a somersault, and lay still.

"I know now why you won the gold crossed-rifle badge," observed Kop-a quietly.

"That's a stroke of luck!" said Zack. "And the wind blowing so no one could hear! It means rabbit stew to-night." He looked at his watch. "There's just ten minutes left of our noon stop. Let's see what Ruff would do on your trail if we should become separated. Where is he now?"

"Asleep in the bag. He's all in. Thinks he's been helping Barry pull."

"Then give me your mitten. Walk over to the boulder and keep out of sight. Don't call or make a sound and we'll see if he can pick up your scent."

Ruff, pulled out of the bag, blinked sleepily and growled considerably upon being awakened. It was the first time Zack had handled him and his back fur rose instantly. But he forgot his displeasure as he looked about and failed to see Kop-a. Dismay and bewilderment showed plainly in the small black face and his growls ended in a cry as he began to run about the sled in search.

"Here, Ruff, here . . ." and Zack leaned down with Kop-a's mitten. "Go find Kop-a, go find Kop-a."

Ruff's voice rose in a wail. For the past few days, Kop-a had not been out of his sight. Perched upon an icy hummock with his head back, the dog gave way to his anguish. Susie, watching, gave an answering cry, but Ruff continued until Zack thrust the mitten under his nose once more.

"Come over here, Ruff," coaxed Zack, and the puppy, wagging his tail halfheartedly, followed in the direction of the boulder. After a few patient attempts on Zack's part, the puppy began to run in circles until he discovered Kop-a's scent. Whining softly in his excitement, his tiny black body disappeared among the hummocks. Shrill barks of joy soon announced his discovery of the boy behind the boulder.

"Next time he'll know even sooner what to do," said Zack. "He's quick . . . quicker than most puppies. It'll be a game with him after a while. But let's get started . . . time's up. E. B. said there's a cabin near some falls at the head of the lake. Maybe we can reach it tonight."

With the aid of compass and maps, Zack arrived at the head of Ivory Horn Lake, which was joined to a still larger lake by a swift turbulent river coursing through a connecting gorge. Water, black and deep, raced through this rocky roadway, pouring itself with a constant roar over a cliff as it entered Ivory Horn. A shelf of ice, tasseled with long icicles, extended over the falls, showing where the original line of freezing had been before the water was released. Narrow in width and slippery, this shelf appeared to be the only bridgeway in sight. The lake stretched beyond, a solid expanse of white, dotted here and there with willow-covered islands. Day was rapidly fading as Zack kicked open the door of a cabin on an embankment at the edge of the falls.

The timber of the cabin had evidently been floated down the river from the sea, for it was without bark and of a peculiar gray smoothness. The roof had been covered with tar paper which now, ragged and torn, blew in the wind with a rattling sound. Within, the air was damp and musty. A squirrel, chattering and scolding, scampered outside through a hole in the rough wooden floor. Rusty cooking pans, covered with cobwebs, hung from the walls, and spruce boughs, brown with age, lay in two bunks.

The stove in the cabin was unlike any Kop-a had ever seen. An empty gasoline drum had been bedded in a square frame of wood, which was filled with small rocks and pebbles gathered from the river bottom. The oven was a rusted iron barrel, its chimney made of many tomato cans neatly patched together. A little iron shutter, pulled by a chain, acted as ventilator. Driftwood was stacked close by, while on the wall, directly facing the person who warmed himself at the unique stove, was a photo gallery of smiling ladies of the silver screen.

"Some old hermit lives here," said Zack, "someone who liked movies when he lived Outside. Cast your eye on that stove! It's a work of art! We might as well burn up that old spruce and save the firewood. I'll put on water for the stew. Hello, here's a note," and Zack removed a piece of paper from the back of the door. The message was printed in pencil and addressed to "Jim."

"Don't try to cross on the ice shelves. They won't hold. I'm starting now to try out the lake ice. See you on the other side. Close the door tight when you leave.
Sandy McArdle

In the fast graying light, Zack and Kop-a looked at one another. They could hear the steady downpour of the falls and the flap of loose tar paper on the roof.

"I guess no one stopped for that note," said Zack in a hushed voice. "Poor Sandy never made it, I'm thinking. I'll have to report this case at headquarters. The paper is growing yellow. It was probably written just about a year ago. This cabin is off the beaten trail and if anyone did stop, it might have been someone who couldn't read. I was planning to try out that shelf in the morning."

"Would the dogs have gone over that narrow ledge?" asked Kop-a. He felt a bit shaken and glanced about the cabin, somewhat awed by the thought of Sandy McArdle's untimely ending. Moreover, his eyes had caught sight of an old brown sweater hanging on a nail on the further side of the door. The sleeves of the sweater were bent at the elbow as though Sandy had just slipped his arms out of them.

"They'd come if I went ahead," answered Zack. His own eyes followed Kop-a's and discovered the sweater. "Oh, Sandy may have made it all right," he said casually.

"Probably a good old sourdough, the kind that lives forever. Built himself another cabin farther on and we may meet him yet. Anyway, we're welcome to what's here, I guess. We needn't disturb anything, for after all, this is Sandy's cabin. He might be coming home again some day."

Zack changed the subject abruptly. "You know, I like that old stove. I believe I'll make some biscuits. Good old-fashioned soda biscuits and rabbit stew. How's that? You feed the dogs and put them to bed in that lean-to out there and I'll skin the rabbit. Hot biscuits and stew!"

"Sounds great," said Kop-a, responding to the cheerful note in Zack's voice.

"And then you'll say 'Ah-nee-kah-h.' " Zack rubbed his stomach with one hand and rolled his eyes toward the roof as he drawled out the words between ecstatic sighs. "Do you know what it means in Eskimo?"

" 'Oh, my! Isn't that nice!' " Kop-a mimicked Zack's voice. The boy was laughing now, all trace of depression gone. "I ought to know . . . they were the very first words I learned in Eskimo!"

The rabbit stew and hot biscuits were all Zack had promised. That night, for the first time in many months, the single window of Sandy McArdle's cabin shone with light and warmth upon the dark and ceaseless falls outside. Within, Ruff stretched his short length in utter content before the barrel-oven while Zack and Kop-a, their heads close together, studied maps and planned their journey to the coast.

"Are we making good time?" the boy asked Zack anxiously. "Could we go any faster? I'm feeling a lot better. I scarcely cough at all."

"We're making average time," Zack told him. "After we cross the lake, perhaps we'll hit a trail of some sort. You do seem a lot better but there's no use killing yourself by hurrying. Is it so awfully important? Perhaps sometime you'll feel like telling me more . . ."

"I know," said Kop-a, nodding his head hastily, "I must seem like a piker. You've been . . . you've been a brick. I'd like to talk . . . but I can't. Maybe when we're nearer the coast . . ."

CHAPTER TEN

Crossing Ivory Horn Lake

THE following day dawned a pleasant one and before Kop-a was awake, Zack had gone down to the lake and chopped a hole in the ice with the chisel E. B. had given him.

"This is a handy thing!" he told Kop-a as he entered the cabin and found the boy stirring oatmeal over the fire. "The pole measures the depth of the ice after you have cut through with the knife. The ice is three feet deep out here and fairly solid. I believe we'll make it all right."

"Any chance of catching some fish?" asked Kop-a. "What would anyone catch in this lake, anyway?"

"Trout, whitefish, grayling, suckers . . . I wish we had time to find out. I'd like to broil some fish over these coals and serve it with a crisp strip of bacon on the top."

Throughout the meal Zack was thoughtful and spoke but little. After his second cup of coffee, he rose and stood looking down at the boy.

"You know, I don't care so much for myself, but I'd hate to have you get a ducking. In a way, I'm responsible for you. Would you rather stay here and let me try it out . . ."

"I guess not!" There was earnest indignation upon

Kop-a's face as he looked up. "No, sir, I'm going wherever you go. You said last night that we'd share fifty-fifty."

"All right." Satisfied with what he read in the boy's face, Zack turned away. "I just wanted to make sure how you felt. Do you know much about candling ice?"

"Not much. Of course I've heard and read about it. The ice crashes all of a sudden, doesn't it?"

" 'Crashes' is the word, all right. It's not like regular ice. It's a mass of splintered needles and has no body. One of the gambles of the north."

"Couldn't you hang onto the edge and crawl out?"

"No, not always. As fast as you grab an edge, it's likely to break off. Of course there are always exceptions. You stand a better chance if you can be pulled out. But the big danger is the air space between the ice and the current. Most of the lakes lower their watermark in the spring and a fellow could float along in the current with a roof of ice over his head and no one know the difference. And he couldn't break through to get out."

Kop-a was silent for a moment. Then, "Mrs. Henry was pretty worried about our crossing this lake, wasn't she?" he asked. "She kept speaking of it."

"Yes, she hears the trappers talk. You see, if we spent time walking around this lake, all the other lakes would be thawed out and we'd have a devil of a time getting out of here. Once the ice starts to go, you have to travel fast. Ivory Horn is the largest on our route. Once we're over, we'll be in the Lost Lands and then we'll have to watch out for squalls. No one wants to live here and I don't wonder!"

"There's something I'd like to ask you," said Kop-a. He spoke with a little hesitancy as if ashamed of what he was about to say, and kept his eyes on the breakfast dishes which he was piling up to wash.

"Spill it," encouraged Zack.

"If you should see Lucas . . . and I don't," he added in a lower voice, "will you tell him I tried to reach him . . . that I did my best. He'll understand . . . I guess that's all."

"I'll tell him," promised Zack. "But I guess if one gets over, the other will. You still don't want me to go first and try it out?"

"And let me sit in the doorway and watch you drown?" Kop-a shook his head. "No, I'm going with you."

"Well, I hope we shall be camped on the other side by to-night. I don't pretend to know this lake, its depths or its currents. We'll take it slowly. Dress warmly and maybe you'd better empty out Ruff's baggage when he isn't looking. He's got enough rocks collected to build a stone wall."

Moise was decidedly reluctant about crossing. He whined, he even wailed at the edge of the shore, his brown eyes seeking his master's, and he followed only when Zack went ahead. Ruff, looking out from the sled bag, peered around with the expression of an irate passenger. His baggage, reduced to one stick and a small stone, did not add to his happiness. King, Lingo, and

Nigak moved forward obediently, but Barry for some reason plumped himself down heavily upon the ice. Susie made no attempt to chastise but stood over him and looked up anxiously into Zack's face.

"What's the matter with you dogs?" asked Zack. "You act like a bunch of old women. They don't like these crossings," he added to Kop-a. "If Moise thought he could fool me, he'd make a big circle and get back to the cabin to-night. Now come on, dogs. It won't be long before we're over. E. B. says there's caribou on the other side." Zack talked naturally in an effort to calm whatever fears the boy might be entertaining as a result of the dogs' reactions. "Mush, boys, mush!"

Moise, submitting to the inevitable, started forward but looked back at the shore frequently. From time to time the team halted as Zack chopped with the bladed end of his pole and then measured the depth of the ice. Whenever in doubt, he lay flat on his stomach to measure, distributing his weight. Farther to the south, one could see the open black waters of a current. Several times their feet shattered the thinly frozen ice over thawed areas and in the suspense which hung over them, the sounds seemed doubly loud.

"If you feel your feet getting wet, climb onto the sled and change into dry socks," called Zack.

"They're all right so far," answered Kop-a.

"It's shallow here," Zack reported. "I can tell by the sound of the current. Come on, Moise, I know you don't approve, but it can't be helped. Buck up, you dogs."

"Have you ever fallen in?" asked the boy curiously. "Is that why the dogs act this way?"

"We've gotten damp now and then," and Zack grinned back good-humoredly. "But dogs just naturally hate cold water."

The little cabin by the falls had become a mere black spot when Zack's sharp eyes discovered a bank of fog to the south. Fog generally meant thaw. But he was more than halfway over now and it was no time to turn back. Soon they were swathed in a world of gray mist. At times it became difficult for the two travelers to see each other. While Kop-a and the dogs waited, Zack, a blurred dark figure, would chop, measure, and then call for them to come forward.

"This won't last long," came his voice through the mist. "We'll have some hot tea once we're over."

The fog lifted almost as suddenly as it had appeared. As they emerged, they found themselves to be three-quarters of the way across. A dark line of trees and low shrubs separated the lake from the horizon.

"Looks like willow and ground birch ahead," said Zack. "Feeding grounds for caribou. I wouldn't mind a nice steak, would you?" he asked. "Or would you prefer fried chicken and waffles?" The tone was light, demanding a smile, and the boy responded, his lips blue.

"Anything hot would do right now."

"Pull your hood down lower," warned Zack sharply, "and keep feeling your face. Feet dry?"

"Yes."

"That's good. There's a wind from the north and we may get a storm later. Beat your arms a little to start the circulation. This isn't such a bad crossing. I've been on worse."

They were but one-quarter of a mile from shore when Zack's chisel cut into the ice with a noisy splintering sound. "We'll go round a bit," he said abruptly, and without further explanation, he led the dogs north of the direct route he had outlined. It was easy to see the shore now. Thickets of willow towered from eight to ten feet in height. A low line of dwarfed birch grew at the head of an inlet still farther north.

Despite their nearness to land, Zack appeared even more cautious. He chopped and measured frequently and talked in a low tone to Moise, who was now in a hurry to reach shore.

"Not so fast, old fellow, not so fast. Just a few more minutes . . . look out!" he yelled suddenly as there was a cracking sound, like the sharp report of a pistol.

Taken by surprise, Kop-a jumped to one side, his hands still grasping the handle bar. But his feet slipped. The sled and dogs seemed to be toppling over him as he slid through space. There was a deafening sound in his ears and at the shock of cold water against his face, his hands automatically let go of the handle bar. The sled, released from his weight, tipped back onto the ice.

Down he sank into the coldest and blackest water he had ever known. It was not deep water, but there were jagged slippery rocks at the bottom. And as he struggled to his feet, gasping and choking, a swift wash of current knocked against his knees. They buckled and he felt his body swept back by its force. Again he struggled to rise and this time his head struck the rough edge of ice just above. The current was carrying him beneath the ice! And in spite of all he could do, he was being pulled farther and farther away from the opening in the ice through which he had fallen. The water tugged and dragged at him as if with unseen hands, and when next he opened his eyes, the sky was gone . . . a rough ceiling of ice was overhead!

Fear, such as he had never known before, left Kop-a paralyzed, helpless. The cold water had now seeped through his heavy clothing and the shock sent excruciating pain up and down his legs. His heart seemed to stop beating. So chilled and numb had his whole body become that he moved with great effort and the sharp points of ice above forced him to keep his head lowered. Time was ticking into eternity . . . his body dead . . . his mind alone remained alive . . .

There was another crash. The ceiling of ice came down about him and something heavy struck him between the shoulders. Another stinging blow glanced across his forehead. An arm like an iron band gripped him and never lessened its hold. Through his numbed senses, it seemed to be life itself, supporting him, sustaining him. It bore him forward against the pulling current and he opened his eyes to glimpse the sky once more. Above the rim of jagged ice ahead waited the blurred dark forms of the dogs, still hitched to the sled which they had dragged back from the water. Something black hung over the edge of the ice.

"Hang onto the reins," shouted Zack in his ear. The vise-like grip released him as Kop-a's hands clutched the reins.

"Mush, Moise, mush!" came Zack's voice from behind. But Moise did not move. He seemed to be transfixed with terror at beholding Zack in the water. Suddenly he crouched low as if ready to spring towards them.

"Moise, Moise!" Zack's voice above the sound of the water was pleading desperately. "Back up! Back up!"

Moise backed, pulling King with him, his eyes on Zack.

"Mush, mush, haw!" Zack's voice rang out. All his remaining strength seemed to go into that cry. Moise leaned forward and the rest of the dogs followed. The sled moved and Kop-a, holding fast to the reins, was lifted out of the water. And the ice held.

"Throw back the reins!" came Zack's voice.

How he managed to get the dogs back to the edge of the ice and throw the reins to Zack, Kop-a never remembered. There was a red film over his eyes and he moved stiffly, with but a single thought in his mind. Zack was in the water . . . Zack must not drown . . . Zack must be pulled out.

"Mush, Moise," he heard his own voice call . . . a voice which seemed to be no part of him. And the sled moved forward for the second time.

Fortunately, it was a quick trip to shore. It did not take Zack long to make a fire of willows in the shelter of a small gully. Although their outer clothing was stiffly frozen, the woolen close to their bodies remained flexible. In quick makeshift changes, they warmed themselves and Zack put up the tent. Once inside, they drank hot tea and crawled into their bags to rest. Even Zack was more tired than he cared to admit.

"It's a good thing it grew dark early," said Zack after

a while. "I'll keep the fire going low all night just to dry us out. I don't believe anyone will see it."

In the excitement, Kop-a had forgotten that they might be watched, now that they had arrived on the other side. Surrounding the tent were clothes and blankets drying, for half of the sled had been submerged. Ruff, in the swinging bag, had received a wetting, but seemed none the worse. He now lay rolled in his deerskin between them.

"It's getting colder," Zack reported after a look at his thermometer. "Feeling better?"

"I'm fine," answered Kop-a. He had been very quiet, assisting when he could, but saying little.

Zack gazed at him inquiringly. "That was a nasty cut you got on your head. I'll wash it out again soon. My feet came down pretty hard on you, I guess."

"So those were your feet!" exclaimed Kop-a, suddenly aroused. "You must have taken a running jump to break that ice . . ."

"Something had to break it. I couldn't let you float down the river alone, could I?" Zack chuckled. "It was just luck that I hit the spot above your head . . . although it didn't exactly improve your appearance. But this won't be your only ducking if you're going to stay in the north," he added.

"So you didn't fall in . . . You jumped in . . . That was pretty fine of you. I . . . I . . ." Kop-a's voice trailed off into silence.

"Nothing to it," said Zack easily. "Just part of my job. That wind has gone down and I guess the storm has veered in another direction. I saw some birch from the lake just a short distance above here. I'm rested and I believe I'll crawl out and see if I can't get some better wood than this willow stuff. It burns too fast. I want to cook some dog feed while we've got a fire. By morning we should be dried out and ready to start again. The dogs are asleep and I want you to keep them here. If they get loose, they'll chase caribou." As Zack talked, he dressed hastily.

Kop-a had dragged himself out of his bag with difficulty. His feet felt unbearably heavy and he could not seem to manage them. "I'm coming with you," he said, a note of determination coloring his voice. For some reason, unexplainable to himself, he did not wish to let Zack out of his sight.

"You get back in there," ordered the corporal. "Your job is to stay here and watch the fire and have my tea ready when I come back. You're just over one cold."

He shoved Kop-a gently but firmly toward the sleeping bag and waited until the boy had crawled inside again. It was only because of a sudden dizziness that Kop-a obeyed. But his eyes followed Zack until the tent flap closed behind the tall hurrying figure, and he listened, holding his breath, until he could no longer hear the crunch of Zack's feet upon the snow outside. Lying so, he slept.

Suddenly Kop-a awakened. Some strange dark premonition hung over him. The wind had an eerie sound as it suddenly swept the lake clear of its hard fine snow and flung it ruthlessly against the sides of the canvas tent. In the distance could be heard the wash of the current below the ice on the lake. The thought of its cold darkness caused Kop-a to sink deeper into his sleeping bag in order to shut out the sound. But for Zack's timely plunge, he might be there now with no other sky above him than a ceiling of ice . . . floating . . . floating . . . That was the way poor Sandy McArdle had gone, with no one to help him.

In terror, Kop-a writhed deeper into the bag, telling himself that he was "yellow" to let himself feel that way. That was the word . . . yellow! There was no excuse to justify it . . . not even a cut on the head. And then suddenly Kop-a knew that he was not alone. This conviction so pierced his thinking that his body jerked itself into a sitting position. He opened his eyes and stared unbelievingly before him.

In the doorway of the tent, their faces almost hidden by the wolverine fur of their parka hoods, stood Mat and Joe Michaud.

CHAPTER ELEVEN

Squall in the Lost Lands

ZACK, with a hatchet at his belt and a rope slung over his shoulder, felt a rise of spirits as he strode north in quest of firewood. Kop-a was safe, he told himself with satisfaction . . . dozing by now in his sleeping bag back in the tent. The great flat frozen expanse of Ivory Horn Lake had been crossed at last and one of their most hazardous undertakings finished.

Zack found himself wishing he could let the Henrys know how game Kop-a had been. Not a cry as the ice cracked like the sound of gunfire beneath him, not a murmur as he had pulled stiff frosty clothing from his shivering body and submitted to having his head treated and bandaged. Yes, the Henrys would be glad to know, though dismayed at the experience. A little sleep, a hot dinner, and Kop-a would be restored to his normal health. The cut on his head was not serious, but might leave a scar. Yes, the boy was game all the way through, Zack mused to himself.

From a distance, the Lost Lands seemed Paradise compared to the barren plains they had just crossed. Thickets of alder and willow lined the river gullies leading to a plateau beyond. Spruce shadowed the distant ridges. It was a welcome contrast, this appearance of something green and living, and Zack stopped to gaze through his binoculars from a high bluff along the lake's shore. Caribou, coming down from the plateau, would linger in small valleys like these to feed upon the tender leaves in spring. A few well-aimed shots and there would be enough red meat for Kop-a, the dogs, and himself until their journey was done.

The Lost Lands! Beyond the plateau would be trackless muskegs and shallow lakes. Lands shunned by natives, except for hunting, and used as a refuge by outlaws. A hiding place for the "bad hats" who wished to escape imprisonment at Stony Mountain or Pond's Inlet. This was the land where a human being, living in the company of wolf and bear, became more beast than man.

It was from the Lost Lands that Inspectors Stamm and Alling had brought out their prisoner, a poor gibbering wretch, gone mad with loneliness. And it was here that Sergeant Logan, dressed as an Indian, had trailed and captured the murderer of Carter, a prosperous trader. Both cases had been recorded in the annals of the Force. And somewhere in this wilderness was the lawbreaker sought by Zachariah Denny.

Spring would not bring his man to the valleys for caribou. In all likelihood, his caches were filled to overflowing with stolen deermeat. But loneliness, a longing to keep in touch with the outer world, a meeting now and then with confederates, would bring him out of his hiding place. He had last been seen fishing at the northern end of Ivory Horn.

"He's a tricky one," Inspector Troland had told Zack at Aklavik, "and you will have to be tricky yourself to catch him. Don't let him charm you into his traps!"

Zack straightened his shoulders and walked faster. So much depended upon this trip . . . the solving of Lucas Joules' problem, and a possible promotion in rank.

Ptarmigan croaked from the tops of distant willows as Zack's feet followed the outline of an old trail made by caribou years ago. There was no sign yet of the little forest of birch which he had spied from the lake that morning. Perhaps he would see it from the bend ahead. Already he was beginning to feel a bit uneasy at having left Kop-a alone. If Mat and Joe Michaud had crossed by the mountain trail, they would probably be at the southern end of the lake by now . . . a half day's travel away. He decided to go a little farther, at least as far as the bend, and then turn back. For company, if nothing more, he wished he had brought Moise with him. But the dog's enthusiasm for hunting would have advertised his whereabouts far and near. Good old Moise! In spite of his fright, the dog had used his head and helped to save their lives that day.

Having reached a slight rise, Zack looked down upon a long narrow inlet. At its very end grew the small forest of birch which he had seen when crossing the lake. The very same! A few blows of the hatchet, the wood tied together and slung over his back, and he would head for home. Home! It was wherever he pitched his tent. In a few hours clothes would be dry and the dog mash cooked. The flames of the fire would be hidden in the hollow where they camped and smoke would not be seen at night. Morning would find them ready for the day's march and no time lost.

Already he was running toward the trees, following

the shoreline rather than the ice of the inlet. One ducking a day was enough. He was stiff from his plunge in the lake and decided to take no further risks with candling ice. It was better to run on land and limber up. The wind from the lake seemed to be pushing him along, sending a fusillade of snow against his back. Strange, but he seemed to come no nearer the trees in spite of his haste. And then he remembered the absence of perspective in the north. The gray-white snow offered no contrasts to the human eye. A small mouse might take on the proportions of a musk ox . . . a polar bear might resemble a squirrel in this twilight.

Again the wind came sweeping over the lake, singing in a low undertone, and the little birch trees, nearer now, swayed in rhythm toward the ground. Zack stopped and gazed uneasily about him, suddenly reminded of being in the squall country. The wind was gaining in power . . . should he turn back? In ten more minutes he would have the firewood and be on his way. Would ten minutes, maybe less, make any difference? Moreover, he argued, the wind might die down. Taking careful note of his surroundings, Zack hurried on.

Suddenly the wind swept down upon the little inlet, tearing boisterously after Zack. And the wild beating of snow against his back began again. But he had reached the trees. Taking his hatchet from his belt, he was about to strike a blow when the third onslaught of wind came. Now Zack knew he was facing one of the Ivory Horn Lake squalls . . . weird, unpredictable storms of sudden twists and fury!

Screaming shrilly, the wind tore past him and would

have lifted him off his feet had he not twined both arms about the trunk of a sturdy birch and lain flat in the snow, his head downward. Would Kop-a be frightened? Would the tent remain fastened to its staples? The squalls were said to finish as quickly as they began. At any moment it might be over, he told himself, and clung more closely to the tree, clasping his arms tightly together to keep the snow from blowing down his sleeves. Acting on another thought, he decided to hold to the tree with one arm and chop some saplings which were within reach. One by one, he would cut them down and thrust them under his body to act as a mattress and lift him from the cold snow. Later he would burn them as firewood.

The wind, streaming past him, venomous in its fury, seared his face like a hot iron. But he continued to chop . . . one . . . two . . . three . . . four blows . . . and into the fifth went all his strength. The young tree toppled but before he could catch it with his mittened hand, the wind swept it up out of his reach, and then out of his sight. He looked after it, surprised and a little bewildered. A small thing to happen, but it frightened him. He was helpless against this wind! Vexed at his failure, he selected another sapling. His hands were aching and stiff with the cold and, as if they were no longer a part of himself, he watched them slowly grasp the handle of the hatchet. But his fingers were too numb to retain their hold. The hatchet fell from his hand and slid along the snow a little distance from him. Again he was conscious of that flash of fear. Above all things, he must keep his hands and feet warm!

With icy fingers he managed to loosen the rope from his back and shoulders, sling it around the trunks of two trees, and laboriously tie the two ends about his waist. Now that his body was held fast, he was able to warm his hands against his chest. But his whole body was cold and the seriousness of his predicament swept over him with alarming force. He knew he must act and act quickly if he wished to live. To lie there meant certain death . . . he must keep moving! What a fool he had been not to turn back at the very first warning of the wind!

His only choice now was to go back to the shore line and follow it to the tent. He would crawl on his hands and knees if need be, but at least he would be moving and keeping his blood in circulation. Later he would come back for the firewood. Summoning his strength and bent nearly double, he faced the wind, picked up the hatchet and took a few steps forward.

Just at that instant the snow, as if poured from the sky, came seething down. The wind had been bad enough, but now this! It was no use; the snow blinded him and the wind hurled him backward.

He re-entered the little forest of birch and lay flat once more, telling himself that he would wait until the storm was over. But how long would the storm last? Could he hold out against the drowsiness which would inevitably follow soon? Was this to be the end of all he had planned? Stamm, Alling, Logan . . . they had encountered these storms and lived to tell about them. Was he, Zack Denny, to go down in the annals of the Force as deceased, frozen to death when only on the border of the Lost Lands? Was he finished and only beginning to realize it now?

This last question drove him to his knees, hugging the birch trees with one arm while he reached for his pistol. While he could still use his left hand, he would fire the pistol three times . . . a call for help. It was a matter of discipline, of training. And then he would walk, if it took his last breath. To lie there and die was not the way of the Force.

There was no sensation in the finger which pressed the trigger of the pistol. Three shots rang out, lost in the roar and screech of the storm. A feeble gesture, but he was grasping at straws. Straining his ears, he listened for some answer. But it was hopeless . . . hopeless to expect any living human being to hear him. He struggled to his feet and fired three more shots.

Zack was battling for his life now, and for all that he loved. So much depended upon his return. Kop-a would be waiting . . . the Henrys . . . his friends at the post. Their unwritten law . . . "Do not let down the Force!" All these thoughts flashed through his mind in rapid succession.

A gust of wind threw him to his knees but he rose once more, steadying himself by holding to the branches of the trees. He seemed to be pushing against a wall. Summoning all his remaining strength, he staggered forward. But his legs were lifeless and collapsed beneath him. He sank, huddled at the foot of the birches, as the rope, whipped by the wind, soared into space like some living thing. And then the drowsiness which he dreaded came at last, closing down upon him slowly, surely, shutting out the storm, dulling the pain in his body.

From a great distance, calling him back, came the sound of shrill, sharp yelping. Was he dreaming? No, it was coming nearer. Was it Moise? No, Moise did not bark like that. Nearer . . . louder . . . His left arm, slow and stiff, made a desperate attempt to reach his pistol but it was too late. A lean gray shadow hurled itself upon him from out of the whirling snow. Sharp teeth tugged at the throat of his parka and tore at his mittened hand as he tried to protect his face.

And strangely enough, he heard once more Inspector Troland's voice as it sounded the morning he left Aklavik. A voice which repeated itself, like the retracing of a needle upon a cracked phonograph record. "Go ahead, my boy, but be careful . . . it's a wild country . . . it's a wild country . . . it's a wild country . . .

Then all sound ceased.

The next thing Zack became conscious of was the fishy smoke of seal oil. It stung sharply in his nostrils, bringing him to the realization that he was alive. There was feeling in his arms and legs. The storm, the birches, the cold and then the gray animal which had sprung at him . . . in spite of them, he was alive! Opening his eyes, he saw that the air overhead was full of bluish-white smoke and a light, probably from an oil lamp, came from his right. Above was the curved roof of a snow igloo, the blocks fitted tightly together and sealed with an icy coating. Where was he?

Closing his eyes, he feigned unconsciousness until he

could adjust himself. Caution, born of his training, held him in check. How long had he lain there? How was Kop-a managing without him in this wild storm? For he could still hear the wind as it whistled overhead.

Someone just beyond the light at his right was cooking something and humming a queer little French song under his breath. An Eskimo would not sing a French song but an Eskimo would have built this igloo, perfect in its construction. The gray animal must have been this person's dog and the igloo must be near the birch grove. Then his six shots had been heard after all. At the time, how hopeless it had seemed to fire them! But now he was here, under a shelter and alive. No, Zack Denny was not finished yet. But he would not be able to rest until he got back to Kop-a. It was an obligation which kept pounding at the back of his consciousness.

A tiny hole in the roof acted as ventilator but it was not large enough to clarify the smoky air which was strangling him. And Zack was unable to stifle a gasping cough. Immediately he turned his head, reaching through force of habit for the second revolver which he carried in an inner pocket. The gun was not there.

A slight dark-skinned man, clothed in a fawnskin shirt and deerskin trousers, sat cross-legged before a primus stove, turning some cakes in a kettle of oil. Eskimo doughnuts! Apparently he had just finished his task for there was a pile of cakes stacked in a cracker tin near by. With a deft twist of the wrist, he tossed the last one into the waiting tin and then glanced up quickly to meet Zack's eyes.

"Ah," said the stranger, with a slight gesture of greeting, "you feel better, my frien'? Yes." And before Zack could answer, he sprang to his feet, quick as a panther, graceful as a ballet dancer, and picked up a kettle of snow which he placed on the stove. "We will have tea," he announced with exaggerated graciousness. "These cakes," snapping his fingers in the direction of the doughnuts, "are not for white men."

Zack had a fleeting glimpse of something blue upon the man's wrist. Long hair, coal black, fell below his ears, which were pierced with gold loops. His hair was greased and brushed back, giving the thin face a fox-like expression. Nothing seemed to escape his black, restless eyes.

The igloo was gradually clearing of smoke. Zack felt no desire to move; his body was stiff and sore and the walls before him danced up and down when he moved his head quickly. Though his hands ached and burned, he knew from previous experience that they had not been completely frozen. For a little while it would be well to appear even more ill than he felt, until he could get his bearings and make sure he could stand upon his feet.

His swarthy host had been rummaging in a box and brought out two tin cups. "You have had a narrow escape, my frien'. It is a puzzle to me to know where you came from, alone and without dogs. A herder? No. It is re-mark-a-ble my dog Anore found you in time. He is a wild one, that beast. For-tu-nate-ly, your parka protected you."

There was another flash of blue at the man's wrist as he pushed his hair back from his face. A bracelet! Could it be . . . ? In his excitement Zack almost sat upright but controlled himself with an effort. The stranger was speaking again and the corporal listened intently to the words spoken perfectly but in a labored manner.

"Soon we shall have tea. Yes? Maybe you can sit up? I wonder. Perhaps you crossed the lake . . . or did you come over the mountain? As we become frien's, maybe you will tell me your name? Yes. Ah, the water boils."

Zack, grateful for this one-sided conversation, had been looking about him meanwhile. He saw that he was lying upon a flat shelf of snow which was covered with very fine skins. Two highly polished guns rested against the wall by the low block door and just opposite him lay a large pile of pelts with a braided whip coiled upon the top. Various boxes were heaped upon the floor as if they had just been unloaded from a sled. His host seemed to be well equipped, even prosperous. Zack spoke for the first time, keeping his voice low.

"You heard my signals?" he asked.

"Ah, yes," answered the stranger. "You were almost at my door. I told Anore to find you." There was no reference to the missing revolvers, but Zack felt certain the man had seen him reach for his pocket.

This was no ordinary thief! The man was different from anyone Zack had ever seen. The bracelet and the labored English, the long hair and the dramatic gestures . . . He would bide his time. And meanwhile, he would be gaining strength.

"I'm much obliged to you," said Zack, meaning it sincerely. The stranger waved his hand as if accustomed to saving people's lives, and whistled softly as he made tea.

The beverage, hot and of good flavor, gave Zack new courage. But he sipped it slowly as if every movement were an effort, and finally sank back upon his bed with a stifled groan and closed his eyes, feigning sleep. The stranger watched him carefully and took the cup from his hand. It was then that Zack saw something which made him furious with indignation. The stranger was wearing *his* wrist watch! Controlling his anger, he remained silent, wondering how many steps it would take to reach the guns by the door. But if the guns were not loaded . . .

Just as he opened his eyes to measure the distance, something reddish-brown leaped from one of the boxes. Like a flash it crossed the floor of the igloo and perched upon the clothes dryer.

"Ha, Molly, you're awake," said the man.

Zack stared at the scene before him. It was almost incredible! At first he had only hoped . . . but now the little red squirrel had convinced him. Such a thing could never happen again in a hundred years! The blue bracelet, the labored but perfect English, the soft skins and now the tame squirrel! To think he should stumble, half frozen and quite by chance, into the presence of the very man he had come to find . . . Jean . . . one of the most notorious characters of the north and the brother of Mat and Joe Michaud! Jean Michaud . . . alias Andre Angola!

CHAPTER TWELVE

A Battle of Wits

WHEREVER Jean Michaud traveled, there were feuds among the Eskimos and Indians, empty caches and traps along the trails. Like a will-o'-the-wisp, he managed to escape the law, his two brothers Mat and Joe coming to his rescue when necessary.

The three Michaud brothers came from a strange mixture of bloods . . . Russian, Portuguese, French, and Indian. Jean was said to speak all four languages. More ambitious than his brothers, he had received some schooling in Canada, read considerably, and had toured the States on a vaudeville circuit as a trainer of seals under the stage name of Andre Angola. Later he returned to the north coast where he trapped and traded furs. Here he became interested in witchcraft. At first it amused him to practice among the Eskimos and Indians and then he began to depend upon it to supply his needs. A ritual, muttered over the empty jaws of a trap brought to him by some gullible trapper, was said to fill that trap quickly and profitably, and Jean shared the spoils with the trapper. Bullets dipped in wolverine's blood aided the hunter, and Jean had fresh meat brought to his door. Fish-nets viewed by a whale's eye preserved in alcohol were blessed with fish and Jean's dogs were amply and cheaply fed. Strangely enough, some of the charms worked, but when they failed, Jean, still calling himself Andre Angola, moved farther down the coast. It was an easy way of living and Jean enjoyed its dramatic side. It pleased him to wear jewelry and appear mysterious, like the magicians of the vaudeville stage.

It was the Eskimos who suffered most at Jean's hands. The skin of the little white fox, who lived on drifting ice floes off the coasts, brought high prices from the traders Outside. Jean demanded many fox skins in payment for his witchcraft, and the Eskimos paid, not daring to displease him. Jean had prospered until a few educated Eskimos, Lucas Joules among them, objected and Jean was forced to flee. Zack had learned all this from Lucas' letters and from Inspector Troland at Aklavik. It was their opinion that it was Jean who was now rustling reindeer from the herds a few miles from the coast. Simple herders would be like putty in his hands, would cooperate whether they wished to or not.

There was one small animal which had escaped Jean's greed in the fur trade. It was the little red squirrel. Because of some superstition, he refused to trap or kill this kind of squirrel, and called down afflictions on those who did. Squirrels were said to sense this strange protection and a number of them lived in the roof of his cabin somewhere in the Lost Lands. One or two always traveled with him on the trail.

How true the words of Inspector Troland: "You will have to be tricky yourself to catch him." Zack knew now there was only one way for him to take Jean prisoner and that was to outwit him. Although he felt certain he could stand on his feet, he knew he was not physically able to cope with the witch doctor. But if the storm continued, he could afford to lie there, regain his strength quietly, and then take Jean by surprise.

Kop-a was his greatest worry. If the tent had blown away, the boy would be no better off than he himself had been a few hours ago. On the other hand, should he confront Jean too soon and be outdone, the boy would be left alone in a strange country and at the mercy of Mat and Joe. Carefully turning over every angle of the situation, Zack fell asleep, more exhausted than he realized.

Jean, comfortable in his sleeping bag spread upon a pile of skins, remained awake for some time. Now and then he examined his wrist watch and studied the man just across from him. He seemed perplexed and disturbed and apparently could come to no decision. Finally he, too, fell asleep, and there were no sounds in the igloo but the breathing of the two men and the snap of a twig as the squirrel turned in her sleep or dug deeper into her nest in the box.

Morning dawned clear and cold. Zack made no effort to rise although he felt able to do so. He drank some tea and ate the bacon which Jean brought him and sank back on his bed as if overcome by stupor. Jean, evidently content to have his prisoner quiet, polished his guns, played with Molly and finally mended a broad yoke of beadwork upon a caribou parka. With painstaking care he filled in the torn design with matched beads from a box and then tried on the coat, preening himself like a peacock. He did not appear to be in any particular hurry and seemed to be unaware that Zack was watching him. Outside the dogs howled occasionally and ducks flew overhead.

For the noon meal, Jean cooked some caribou. Zack, watching him, wondered how much Jean had surmised about him. His revolvers bore no marks to identify him with the Mounted Police and he was dressed as an ordinary traveler in those parts. However, a certain tense wariness was evident in Jean's manner. He seemed to be expecting someone, for frequently he turned his head and cast a swift look at the low door of the igloo. The tin of Eskimo doughnuts had remained uneaten. Had they been fried especially for the expected newcomer?

"Your dinner, my frien'," and Jean passed Zack his meat with a theatrical bow. Zack sat up in a dazed fashion on the edge of the snow couch, cut his caribou with a jackknife and drank his tea. The meat was tender and delicious. Knave that he was, Jean was a good cook.

The red squirrel hung about Jean's plate, chattering and helping herself to the tiny portions of meat which he cut and cooled for her. Once she ran with a good-sized piece back to her nest, returned with a nut of some kind and ate it upon Jean's shoulder, dropping the dry shell into his plate below. Then in one leap, she jumped to the plate's edge to eat more meat, chattering all the while. And when she chattered, she jerked her tail vigorously.

Zack knew that he must act soon before a possible third party arrived. At any moment, seeing his strength return, Jean might decide to bind his hands and feet. One careless move on Jean's part, one lax moment off guard, and Zack would spring. Suddenly his eyes lighted on the braided whip now on top of one of the boxes. "Missouri," a fellow constable at Regina, had shown him tricks with a lariat. Why hadn't he thought of it before?

"Have you had the squirrel a long time?" asked Zack casually. It was a good idea, he thought, to keep up a normal conversation until his chance at escape should present itself.

"I found her in a trap. She was young. The man who owned the trap lost his leg later." Jean's voice was harsh with feeling and there was an ugly expression about his mouth. Zack wondered if Jean had called down dark evils upon the man.

He stretched his legs and pushed gently against the floor. They were strong enough, he was sure. Five steps and he would be near the whip. A swift throw, a turn of the wrist, just as he and "Missouri" used to practice with a lariat around the stump of an old tree . . .

Speaking calmly, and still feigning interest, Zack inquired, "The squirrel is more intelligent than other animals, isn't it?"

"The squirrel belongs to the gods. It is a Scan-di-na-vi-an truth."

Jean spoke with the manner of one who had acquired much knowledge, not to be disputed. The blue bracelet was in sight now. It was an ornate affair with an Indian design.

Jean was still eating. For a slight man, he had a tremendous appetite and took his food in large pieces, although he paused between bites to feed the squirrel.

Unseen by Jean, Zack with one hand cautiously unbuckled his belt and put down his plate and cup as if he had finished. Suddenly he rose to his feet, bending forward to protect his head from the sloping roof above.

"Want to see if I can use my legs," he announced, swaying unsteadily.

Jean pushed aside his plate, his eyes narrowed and alert. One hand reached in back towards a coil of rope.

"Not too good yet," said Zack, lifting one foot and then the other.

"Sit down!" Jean's voice rang sharply, although one cheek bulged with a chunk of meat. "Sit down!" he ordered a second time, his eyes now angry.

Zack sat down. There was no use irritating Jean at the moment. His legs had proved to be steady enough. He would act later.

Jean let go of the rope and resumed his eating, though his gaze returned to Zack frequently with a calculating expression. Zack knew now that it would be but a question of minutes before Jean would attempt to bind his hands and feet with rope. He waited until the outlaw took an unusually large mouthful and then rose to his feet the second time. Jean was up instantly. The agility of the man was amazing!

"What's the harm?" asked Zack innocently. "My legs are cramped. What are you so jittery about?" He swayed forward, crooking his right leg and straightening it again. "You've taken my guns. Remember?"

Then, as if losing his equilibrium, Zack swayed toward the middle of the igloo. The whip was within reach. Jean had taken a step backward, his hands extended for the rope. In another moment, he would stoop over . . .

"Say, that whip's a beauty," Zack observed, picking up the long braided lash. "Nice carving." He pointed at the ivory handle.

"Let the whip alone!" came from Jean who had advanced a step nearer, the rope in one hand. His dark eyes had an ugly light in them, and the piece of meat still in his cheek gave his face a distorted appearance.

Zack shrugged his shoulders as if he could not understand Jean's unwarranted concern and put the whip down. He had turned to move away when the igloo was filled with a piercing screech. Molly had burned herself on a piece of hot meat! Jean, startled, turned to look at her when he felt something encircle him, like narrow bands of steel. Twice, the braided thongs of his own whip spun around him with a soft whirring noise and pinned his arms tightly to his sides!

Molly, frightened, leaped for her box as Zack jumped, landing full force against Jean and knocking him to the floor. The meat, forced down Jean's throat, choked him. He gasped for breath; his feet kicked in all directions, knocking the tins from the stove with a loud crash and upsetting the clothes drier.

The two men struggled violently, each battling for his very life. In his weakened condition, Zack might have been overcome but for the fact that Jean could not get his breath. The meat had stuck fast in his throat and tears were blinding him. With his belt, Zack finally managed to lash the outlaw's two feet together. He then turned Jean on his stomach and thumped his back until the meat was disgorged. Panting heavily and weak in his knees, he tied his opponent's arms to his sides with the rope which Jean would have used on him. Then, rising to his feet, he wiped the perspiration from his forehead and made his way to the snow couch where he sat down heavily. It had been a close call and had taxed him severely. But his man lay on the floor, bound and helpless, a prisoner of the Royal Canadian Mounted Police, captured by the coils of a whip, used as a lariat.

"Thanks, 'Missouri,'" said Zack softly, between breaths. "And you, too, Molly," he added to the little squirrel as she scolded noisily, watching him from her box.

Two hours later, Zack reached the shore of Ivory Horn Lake. Jean's four dogs, small-hipped and great-chested, made a magnificent team, hitched single file in elaborately braided harness. The sled with its wicker seat and back, like the spread tail of a peacock and so symbolic of Jean's vanity, held considerable cargo. Jean, bound hand and foot, silent and sullen, rode in the seat, dressed in his bead-trimmed parka. His long narrow face resembled a fox's more than ever as he peered out from his wolverine-bordered hood.

Molly rode in her box beside him. The sled was packed with other boxes, pyramided in the middle with furs lashed over them. On the very top rode the frozen carcass of a reindeer, found in the snow at the back of Jean's igloo. And slashed deep in one of its stiff cupped ears was the mark of the Buckley herds!

To complete the incriminating evidence, Zack had

found, hidden beneath the pile of fur, a noose of great length evidently used in the lassoing of reindeer. Nearby lay his revolvers. And now with his own watch upon his wrist, Zack seemed little the worse for his experience, except for a torn parka and hands which were slightly swollen and tender. To save his strength he rode upon the runners, the big dogs forging their own way through the heavy snow.

Jean, confined to his sleeping bag, was not enjoying his ride. Overhead whistled and snapped the ivory-handled whip, the whip which had been so carelessly left within reach of the man who now wielded it with astonishing skill. Out of the heavy drifts they pushed until a wind-swept, smooth crust was reached and traveling became much easier.

"Mush, Anore!"

On they sped, past the bend where Zack had first sighted the birch trees. Several times Jean looked back as if surprised at Zack's haste. They hurried past the bluff where Zack had stopped and looked up the river valleys through his binoculars. A few moments later, the corporal was straining forward to glimpse his tent pitched in the hollow below, and felt a little sense of surprise that he could not see it. Of course . . . and he chided himself for his stupidity . . . the dark brown canvas, covered with snow, would appear to be as white as the landscape about it! His anxiety for Kop-a was dulling his senses. He had hoped, however, that by this time he would see the boy coming to meet him. He had expected to hear his name called at any moment.

"Mush, Anore! Mush!"

They were sliding down the slope of the bluff to the level stretch which led to the hollow. Closer . . . closer . . . where was the tent? Had it blown away in the storm as he had feared? A clean flat surface of snow marked the spot where only yesterday they had pitched camp. The boy, the tent, the dogs were gone!

Jean watched sullenly as Zack now ran forward. He had not spoken a word since his capture. Down beneath the soft new snow Zack probed until he came to an older layer of crust. Here were footprints, Kop-a's and his own in compact outlines, made the day before. But coming into the tent from the south were some strange prints, two pairs of feet larger than Kop-a's or his own! Yes, and a little farther away were the broad heavy marks of runners which had rested a few hours and then pulled out to the east. His own sled with the narrow Siberian runners had followed.

But what was the dark stain near the entrance to the tent? Blood? No, it was tobacco juice. Mat and Joe Michaud! They had crossed to the lake by the trail which led over the mountains, in unbelievably quick time!

Something moved in the snow before him. It had almost broken through its small sheltering mound, and was pushing forward in a frantic endeavor to free itself and reach him. There was a faint bark and Zack knelt down to investigate. His hands struck the steel of a chain. Something was at the other end of its short length. It was Ruff who finally looked up at him, his neck fur frozen in a brittle collar, his hind legs stiff and dragging. Ruff, who filled the air with joyous cries!

CHAPTER THIRTEEN

Kop-a and the Michauds

KOP-A was very weary when Mat and Joe Michaud called a halt at the end of the first day on the trail. His face burned and his bandaged head throbbed. The Michauds' sled ahead had made no stops for lunch or tea. Jerky was passed around and the journey was immediately resumed across the wide plain. On, on, the two sleds traveled, now dragging through endless white drifts, now slewing with the wind over bare slippery crust.

Joe's heavy, hoarse voice was continually shouting, "Mush! Mush! You fools!" and Mat echoed the same in a higher key when he was not complaining of his cold feet. Would it never end? Where were they going? Up a long narrow river gully they climbed, the dogs fagged and panting, and at last camp was made near a forest of low spruce. Zack's tent and the Michauds' tent were placed close together and the dogs staked at either side. While Kop-a and Joe cut spruce boughs for their beds, Mat dressed and broiled three ptarmigans over a small wood fire.

"Yer might as well eat yer fill, young feller," and Mat gave Kop-a one of the browned birds on a tin plate. "It takes meat to keep yer goin' in this country. Yer folks'll want yer back healthy. The tougher ye be, the more money, I says. It ain't easy ter cart folks 'round when they're spindlin'. Spindlin' nor ugly," he added with a meaning grin which displayed the yellow tooth.

Kop-a took the bird but made no reply and stumbled, blinded by angry tears, towards Zack's tent. Mat's last remark in regard to ugliness referred to Ruff, who had shown uncontrollable hatred of the Michauds when they arrived at Zack's tent the night before. He had growled and barked incessantly and finally, springing at Joe, had sunk small sharp teeth into his thick wrist!

The past twenty-four hours had been a horrible nightmare. Zack's sleeping dogs had not heard the Michauds as they noiselessly approached the tent after Zack's departure for firewood. Kop-a wondered if he would ever be able to forget their evil grinning faces in the doorway of the tent, their white arteegees blending like ghosts with the snow. They had seized Zack's rifle immediately and forced Kop-a to rise and put on his stiff, damp clothes. Without delay, they had overhauled Zack's sled, but were evidently disappointed in what they found. The pages of his diary were written in code and could not be deciphered. Then they questioned Kop-a and threatened him if he did not tell all he knew. But through it all, he had remained silent, scornful.

The storm was terrific. Twice the tent nearly blew away, Mat and Joe gripping it desperately while Kop-a pounded the stakes deeper into the frozen ground. Both Mat and Joe refused to go out and search for Zack as the wind moderated.

"Nothin' doin'," said Joe shortly. "I ain't goin' ter risk my life fer a redcoat."

"Tain't safe," Mat told the boy. "Like as not, this wind'll start agin."

And it was then that Ruff, quick as a flash, had sprung forward and bitten Joe. Plucky little Ruff! Dodging Joe's boot, he had run to Kop-a for safety and looked up into his face for approval. Joe, muttering and scowling, had bound up his wrist in a soiled rag used for cleaning guns.

"No dog can bite me an' live," he told the boy, his eyes threatening. And when they were ready to leave early that morning, Ruff was chained to a stake in the open.

Kop-a, now heating water for tea over Zack's primus stove, went over and over in his mind the scenes which followed, constantly asking himself what Zack would have done in his place.

"Now the pup and yer brass button frien' can go together ter the Happy Huntin' Grounds," Joe had told him as they were ready to start. " 'Cause that's where Denny's headed fer if he ain't there already. No human could stand that storm wi' out a cover. No, I ain't goin' ter look fer 'im an' I don't want ter hear any more from yer," he added emphatically as Kop-a again began to plead with them to search for Zack.

"Mebbe the kid's right, Joe," Mat mumbled timidly. " 'E might be close by, an' arter all 'e's human . . ."

"Shet yer big trap!" roared his brother angrily. "I'm boss and yer'll do as I say! We're travelin' east! If these redcoats think they're so all-fired smart, let 'em prove it! Not another squeak from you, kid, or I'll take over yer dogs an' drive 'em myself. An' I ain't easy wi' the whip, either! I'd make that fat un work!" The end of Joe's lash swung close to Barry's hindquarters. " 'E's lazy and don't earn 'is keep. Now get movin' or I'll blister every one of yer hides! We'll break the trail and you, kid, you follow! An' follow clos't or I'll know why! MUSH!"

The Michaud sled started ahead, Joe's thickset body balancing on the runners and Mat breaking the trail ahead. Once their backs were turned, Kop-a jumped towards Ruff who was straining at his chain and crying piteously. But before he could reach the dog, a lash wound itself about his ankles and he fell forward in the snow.

"What'd I tell yer!" roared Joe, who had stopped. "Jest one more move like that and I'll do yer drivin'."

Helpless, Kop-a had returned to the sled. Again Joe's whip sang out, this time hitting Moise who jumped forward. The other dogs, startled, followed him, and Kop-a barely had time to grasp the handle bar of the sled. Up ahead, he heard Joe laugh. And back of him, growing ever fainter, came the cries of Ruff.

Every step forged ahead seemed traitorous to the friend he was leaving behind . . . the friend who only a few hours before had plunged to his rescue in the icy waters of Ivory Horn. Kop-a kept asking himself: What would Zack have done in his place? Fought hopelessly with his bare fists and then seen the dogs lashed unmercifully by Joe in his driving? No, there would be some better opportunity of escape ahead. But where was Zack now? Was he half frozen, stumbling along the trail, without food, without shelter? And would he finally collapse, exhausted, fall into a stupor, and sleep?

The tea had no flavor and the ptarmigan stuck in his throat. Kop-a pushed his cup and plate aside and leaned wearily against the spruce boughs piled at one side. From the next tent, he could hear the two Michauds smacking their lips noisily over the food and gulping their tea. Sometime later, Joe mumbled something about "the little cur" and Kop-a knew he was examining his injured wrist beneath its soiled bandage. Apparently the wrist was swollen and inflamed. There was a brief silence, followed by a heated argument over the victrola. Mat wanted to amuse himself with some music but Joe forbade him in no uncertain tones.

"Yer big idiot! Don't yer know sounds carry in this air?"

"But the redcoat's done in . . . yer said so yerself," whined Mat.

"Sure 'e's done in, but I ain't takin' no chances jest the same."

Then Joe was not so sure after all that Zack was dead! This admission gave Kop-a his first ray of hope. He forced himself to sit up and eat the ptarmigan which still lay on the plate close by. Though the situation looked hopeless, it would not do to become "spindlin'," as Mat said. In the days ahead he would need every bit of strength, every bit of energy. In spite of obstacles, he had managed to get this far north and he must not lose courage now.

Later, in his bag that night, he did not fall asleep quickly though he ached with weariness. Ruff's cries still sounded in his ears. Zack's dogs had been allowed only two-thirds of their rations and had looked to him for more. . . . Zack's sleeping bag lay unrolled beside him.

In the morning Kop-a felt decidedly better. Joe, on the contrary, was obviously in pain from his now stiff and swollen wrist. Sitting upon the sled, a hunched and disgruntled figure, he did not feel like working, and ordered Kop-a to assist Mat with the loading. It was not an easy task.

When it came time to harness the Michaud dogs, they strained at the tugs, snapped and rolled over, tangling themselves in the reins before they could get started. Mat stung them with the long lash of his whip, and they finally departed up the frozen river gully.

After an hour or so of walking, Joe seated himself upon the Michaud sled and slept, wrapped snugly in furs. His arm was paining him. A little later they stopped by the wayside to heat water and bathe his arm. From then on, it was a succession of stops. During one of these halts Joe sat upright and declared he heard a wolf howl and dogs bark. He was certain Jean must be near, for only Jean could imitate the wolf so perfectly and the sound always made his big dogs bark. Mat, a little hard of hearing, was inclined to believe that Joe was delirious. Kop-a, however, changing the moccasins on King's feet, had heard the same cries and knew that Joe was not mistaken.

Sometimes, after Joe's arm had been bathed, Kop-a noticed that the Michauds would forget to tear down the small windbreak of snow blocks which they built as a shelter for the primus stove. This evidence would be a help to Zack, provided it was he who was following, and not Jean. Moreover, they were now passing through shallow overflows and definite marks of the sleds' runners remained in the snow as they emerged from the water. But most conspicuous of all was the brown tobacco juice which Mat spat from his mouth from time to time. Concern for Joe had made Mat careless. The stains were evident at almost every stop and once Joe complained about them.

"Yer said the redcoat was out o' the way, didn't yer?" Mat reminded him.

Joe, too sick to argue, growled and closed his eyes. The sleds continued on their way, splashing through the overflows and across a plateau, with blue ridges beckoning in the distance.

Some time later, from low brush on the top of a limestone ridge, Kop-a looked down upon a strange section of the Lost Lands. Frozen lakes dotted the level snow plain below, bordered with muskegs and stunted black spruce. Draperies of black and gray lichens hung from the lower parts of the spruce, giving each tree a witch-like and grotesque appearance. Each ridge in the distance, like so many massive waves, looked the same as every other, with canoe birch growing sparsely along its top.

To the north stretched the flat white tundra, with the purple shadows of night gathering on the horizon. Back of him, Kop-a could make out the long rise which they had just climbed, and still farther away in the distance the wide plain they had crossed the very first day. And though the boy strained hard to see, there was not a living person in sight. Nothing moved in that vast expanse of land and sky save a solitary eagle, winging its way southward.

On the side of the second ridge Mat shot a caribou. It was a young animal almost in its prime, and even Joe, drowsy and moaning on the sled, raised himself languidly to look at it. The dogs, fed scantily the night before, turned and watched over their shoulders, drooling at the mouth as Mat removed the choicer cuts of meat.

At the bottom of the second ridge, the travelers pitched camp. After a supper of roasted caribou liver, Joe was put to bed in the Michaud tent. He was feverish and Mat sat anxiously by his side.

Within Zack's tent, Kop-a sat quietly. The second day on the trail with the Michauds had not been as difficult as the first. The frequent stops to heat water for Joe's injured wrist had given him opportunities for rest. He had been able to have hot tea whenever he desired and its warmth revived him. The wound on his head did not ache and he tried to keep the bandage concealed beneath his wool cap. The fewer questions asked, the better. But the thought of the third Michaud brother joining their party had weighed heavily upon him all afternoon. With Jean present, his chances of escape would be lessened. He wondered if Mat, obviously concerned over Joe's illness, would attempt to pursue him if he tried to escape.

At this point, the Michaud dogs broke into an uproar of barking. They were restless and underfed and barked frequently, but the noise never seemed to disturb Mat and Joe. The din gradually subsided and Kop-a, who had dozed lightly, was suddenly awakened by voices in the next tent. Joe was talking, remonstrating with Mat.

"Yer want me ter see if 'e's all right? Course 'e is," whined Mat. "That kid, 'e's skeered. Ain't said a word all day. We don't have ter watch 'im. No gun, no compass, no food . . . 'e'd starve an' now 'e knows the redcoat's dead, same's us. Besides, there's somethin' wrong wi' 'is head. 'E's got a rag tied round it. My feets is tired . . ."

There was a low rumble of Joe's voice and Mat continued. "Well, I'll look an' then I'm quittin'. My feets is cold. More hot water? I jest fixed some." There was a pause as Mat came to the door of the tent and looked out. " 'E's in there. I can see 'im."

A long silence followed. Both of the Michauds must have slept. Again came Joe's deep voice. He talked of hearing the wolf howl and of Jean. Then there were sharp exclamations as he turned in his sleeping bag.

"Ouch! That cussed pup! Too bad I didn't crack 'im off when I had the chanc't. Say, Mat, I'm burnin' up. Gimme a cold drink. Move that bearskin away . . . sometimes it growls and I can see it move. Look! It's movin' now! Think I'm gettin' dippy, Mat? Ouch! My arm! Ain't no feelin' in my fingers. We oughter get ter Jean's by to-morrer. Too bad 'e don't know we're comin'. Wake up, wake up, Mat! Don't yer hear me? MAT! MAKE THAT BEAR STOP GROWLIN'! It's comin' this way. Mat! Mat! Where be yer? Gimme 'nother drink an' I want some more hot water fer my arm!"

So the Michauds were bound for Jean's camp! They would arrive the next day! Kop-a sat up straight, every nerve alert. If he wished to escape, he would have to leave that night. Though he lacked gun, compass and supplies, he would have to go. It was his only opportunity. He must first find Zack, and then together they would reach Lucas. Nothing else mattered now . . . there was so much at stake and so little time!

CHAPTER FOURTEEN

Zack Travels With a Prisoner

ZACK, crossing the wide snow-drifted plain with Jean, following the tracks of the two sleds ahead, did not find his task easy on the first day.

It had become necessary to release Jean from his bondage of rope and sleeping bag for the long trip ahead. If he remained bound so long that his circulation of blood slowed, he would run the risk of freezing his hands and feet, despite the protection of the sleeping bag.

Zack remembered how often he had heard from the lips of his superior officer one of the most stringent, vital demands of the Force: "Bring back your prisoner alive and intact." It was never to be disregarded. Jean Michaud was his prisoner and must be treated accordingly.

"All right, Jean," Zack's voice had been curt as he released Jean from his sleeping bag, "we're following two sleds east." He pointed his mittened hand in the direction of the plain. "You'll keep in front of me and break the trail for the dogs. If you're smart, you'll do as I say. No tricks or funny business or you'll go into the bag again. I shall be checking the trail after you. Now . . . get going!"

And Jean, his sloe-black eyes watchful and his narrow

face twisted with bitter humiliation under the cover of his hood, obeyed in silence. They zigzagged, circled, and fought their way against a stinging wind, always searching for the compressed tracks beneath the white coverlid of snow. Sometimes the tracks lay exposed in wind-swept places; at other times they were forced to probe beneath drifts four and five feet deep.

Wind cut their faces and made them gasp in steamy breaths. But they pushed on, both knowing that the distance had to be covered before they could find relief within the shelter of a gully.

All of Zack's possessions were now in the hands of Joe and Mat Michaud . . . his private papers, police diary, maps, clothing, food, guns . . . even the steel hand- and ankle-cuffs which he might have used to manacle Jean. But these things seemed inconsequential compared to the fact that Kop-a and his dogs were in the Michauds' power. Thinking of his dogs, Zack writhed in mental torture. He had ruled them with a firm hand but always with affection and understanding. They would be startled and bewildered by any act of cruelty. His one comforting hope lay in the thought that perhaps Kop-a was driving. But would the boy be physically able to balance on the runners and manage seven dogs?

Zack turned his glasses frequently on the wide sweep of land ahead. Since they had left the lake, there had been no sign of sleds or men. By this time the Michauds would have gained the cover of one of the gullies which honeycombed the sloping sides of the plateau. He planned to overtake them somewhere in the shadow of the ridges still farther on, making a silent, unseen approach. But now the trail consistently pointed toward the gully at the extreme left. Would this lead to Jean's hide-out? Jean gave no indication of being disturbed except that his eyes constantly scanned the slope beyond. If he was aware of following his brothers, he gave no sign.

Meanwhile Ruff had been petted and fed by Zack, whose indignation knew no bounds at finding the puppy chained, the certain victim of wolverines if not starvation. The trip inside Zack's parka had limbered his stiffened legs and warmed his small shivering body. Later, completely restored, he rode in state, cradled in a most unusual sled bag found among Jean's treasures. The bag was of crimson velvet, dotted with brass star and moon shaped spangles, and edged at top and bottom with ermine tails, a gay and startling reminder of Jean's vaudeville days. Between naps, the tiny dog, standing upright, would gaze out from his celestial trappings and up into Zack's face, his large eyes questioning.

"Yes, we're going to find Kop-a," Zack would reassure him, and then the brass stars and moons would move weirdly about as Ruff's tail thumped hard beneath them. And always before he disappeared into the bag again, he would growl and take a parting nip at some irritating ermine tail within reach. It was not long before the fringe of tails which ran along the top of the bag hung in frozen and distorted shapes.

After grueling work through unusually heavy drifts of snow, Zack would call a halt and make tea behind a shelter of snow blocks. He knew that he must conserve his strength and keep fit for an even greater task ahead, when there would be three Michauds to deal with in place of one. During one of these pauses, Jean spoke for the first time since he had been made a prisoner.

"Why does the Mountie not signal his friends with his pistol?"

So Jean was worrying over the party ahead, wondering if they were also Mounted Policemen! On the other hand, he may have suspected his brothers' presence nearby and hoped that some word from Zack would confirm his suspicions. And in view of what had taken place in the last few hours, it was not surprising that Jean had called him "Mountie." Rather than discuss the party ahead, Zack decided to ignore the question.

"What makes you think I'm a Mountie?" he asked Jean, and was hardly prepared for the tirade of abuse which was instantly unleashed upon him. Jean's voice rose higher and higher as he talked. Towards the end, he fairly screamed in his rage. His hands shook visibly and his black eyes held little points of fire in their depths.

"Bah! Of course you're a Mountie! The way you walk . . . the way you stand! So!" and Jean insolently threw out his chest like a pouter pigeon. "You coppers! How I hate you! How I despise you! You think you own the north, you and your high ways. Guardians of the law! The law . . . bah! I have been asking myself ever since last night, why didn't I leave you to freeze in the storm! Why did I not let A-nore finish you? Why . . ."

"It was your good luck that he didn't," interrupted

Zack quietly. "Of course I'm grateful to you for saving my life. However, I suspect you thought you were helping someone else until you saw I was a white man."

Zack paused and Jean waited, tense and watchful. "Someone who eats Eskimo doughnuts," Zack continued, his eyes on Jean's face. "And when you discovered I was white and a 'copper,' as you call it, you decided to wait for your friend to come before you did away with me. Two could do a better job than one. Right? And meanwhile it pleased you to take my pistols and watch and see me worry a little."

Jean's face was livid now and his mittened hands clenched. "You are so smart it is painful!" His voice rose, shrill and uncontrolled. "Why aren't you all dressed up in your little red coat . . . why don't you wear it under your parka? What's the matter . . . are you afraid? Yes, you are afraid. You are stupid cowards, the whole lot of you, yellow as the stripes on your britches!"

"That's enough, Jean." There was a determined, aggressive glint in Zack's blue eyes. "When it comes to the Force, be a little careful what you say."

Jean's mouth was half open. He would have liked to say more, but for once his wily tongue failed to do his bidding. Strangely uncomfortable, he took the pannikin of tea which Zack handed him.

"We'll wait and see what the judge has to say about the deer over there." Zack nodded toward the frozen carcass on the sled. "Maybe then you'll sing a different tune. The ear has the Buckley mark, I notice. But stealing reindeer isn't all you're wanted for, Jean.

Not by a long shot. For two years you've bedeviled the natives up and down the coast with your charms and taken their supplies under the name of Andre Angola. Andre Angola! That's some name! As Andre Angola, witch doctor, you took Etah's driftwood, for instance. Etah lives alone and he's an old man. He didn't dare refuse you. Lucky his neighbors came along before he froze to death. And how about Jonas? He has eight children to feed and you took most of his seal meat. I could name a lot more. And those beaver huts down below Silver Pond. Someone broke into them last winter."

Jean's long narrow face, passive now, showed no sign that he understood what Zack was saying. The wind had died down for a few moments and the sun shone on the gold and green beads of his parka. They flashed like the iridescent backs of beetles and Jean stroked them with his fur mitten as he drank his tea and stared into space.

"By the way," and Zack's voice was matter-of-fact, "the police over at Aklavik believe you stole Lucas Joules' labret, the green stone his ancestors wore . . ."

"Lucas Joules!" Jean's face was distorted with sudden fury. "So it is Lucas Joules who is scared and sent for you! Yes, I might have known! The dirty-skinned, white-livered Eskimo! Always the preacher! Always the saint! Bah!" He jerked his head convulsively. Zack knew he had touched a vital spot. Jean hated Lucas Joules more than he hated the Mounted Police.

Meanwhile Ruff, aroused by the voices, wriggled about in his spangled bag and finally tumbled out onto the snow. He came running eagerly to Zack to be petted and then began to search hopefully about for Kop-a. Jean's team of giant huskies, aloof but curious, turned their heads to watch him. Ruff was small. His black coat was rough and unkempt. His spindling shanks and thin sharp face were not of their breed and he was looked upon as an intruder.

When his search proved fruitless, Ruff seated himself with a dejected air beside Zack and opposite Jean. This was the first time the puppy had seen Jean at close range and he stared with careful scrutiny, his white ear cocked forward. A growl began to hum in his throat and Jean, still smoldering with anger, suddenly became conscious of the sound. That a mere puppy, and a mongrel at that, should find him objectionable was irritating. And although the puppy almost immediately switched his attention to the squirrel's box upon the sled, Jean could not contain himself.

"The little dog," he broke out nervously, "I do not like him. Why should he stare and growl so all the time? First at me and now at Molly. He is young . . . he should play. But he sits about with the face of an old man. I do not like him."

At that particular moment Molly appeared and seated herself complacently on the edge of her box, jerking her long reddish tail in the sunlight. In a fraction of a second Ruff had caught sight of her and in another instant was in pursuit, running the length of the sled and barking noisily. But before he could reach her, Molly, with neat precision, leaped and landed safely on Jean's shoulders.

Meanwhile Jean had risen to his feet and with astonishing swiftness had seized the squirrel's nest and held it high overhead with both hands. The incident would scarcely have been worth noticing but for the flash of intense fear upon his face. So intense was this fear that Zack found himself pondering over it long after they had continued on their way.

Following the sled tracks, Zack and Jean arrived at the entrance of the farthermost gully late that night. During the day, Jean had offered no resistance, walking ahead of Zack and always in view. He was only too conscious of the loaded pistol which Zack wore in his holster, and he knew that Zack, quick on the draw, would not spare him in a final combat. As they had no tent, Jean was given a snow knife and told to build an igloo. Released from the labor of breaking the trail, he set about it with alacrity and, pleased at being watched, moved about with a peculiar feline grace and jauntiness of manner.

In the gray twilight, Zack watched the operation with interest. Curved blocks, carefully selected from snow of a certain firmness, were arranged in a perfect circle. Row upon row of blocks were added, each row slanting further inward until the walls rose in a rounded dome, the opening at the top becoming smaller and smaller. Jean, working within, gradually disappeared from sight, but the sound of the snow knife could be heard as he chipped, scraped and fitted the white blocks together.

Toward the end, the actor in him could not forego a few dramatic flourishes as though all the world were indeed a stage. Before the last block at the very top was to be slipped into place, he appeared in the small opening, bowed graciously, airily waved an arm, and then withdrew. In another moment, the last block could be seen working into position and Jean came forth again, this time crawling on his hands and knees, using one of the foundation blocks as a door. Loose snow was then packed into cracks and the igloo, perfect in shape and gleaming white beneath a greenish-blue moon, was done.

"The Mountie is sat-is-fied?" asked Jean, waving in the direction of his handiwork. "Ah, yes," he answered himself, and with obvious reluctance returned the snow knife.

After supper, which proved a silent affair, Zack mended his torn parka. Jean sat close to Molly's box while Ruff, leashed to a stake by the clothes drier, kept his distance. And before Jean was bound for the night, Zack allowed him to smoke his pipe, a miniature wolf's skull carved in ivory. Zack lighted it and Jean inhaled and puffed with an elaborate manner, sending out rings of smoke, his gold earrings flashing through his greased black hair whenever he moved his head. Occasionally Ruff's eyes would leave Molly's box and follow the rings of smoke to the ceiling, but they always returned to the squirrel's nest. Molly kept discreetly out of sight. Once in a while she could be heard chattering softly.

Now that Jean's stomach was full and he seemed to be enjoying his pipe, Zack hoped that he would talk a little. From a certain tenseness in his behavior, Zack felt positive that they were in the gully which led to Jean's hide-out. Did Jean now suspect his brothers to be ahead?

"You speak English well, Jean. Where did you study?"

Jean was pleased with the compliment. Flattery seemed to loosen his tongue. "Ah, I have studied in many places," he answered vaguely. "Also I listen . . . I listen care-ful-ly and when I am alone I speak with myself. I am a gen-tle-man, a schol-ar and trainer of seals at heart though I live in this un-ed-u-ca-ted land. A gen-tle-man, a schol-ar and trainer of seals," he repeated and then, as if overcome with his own esteem, he bowed his head silently.

"You are not like your brothers," observed Zack.

"My brothers?" and for the first time, Jean acknowledged he was of the Michauds. "No, I am not like my brothers. Joe is a savage and Mat is a fool."

And then his mood changed swiftly. His mouth was ugly and the little points of fire flashed again in his eyes as he looked at Zack.

"Listen, you. No matter what Jean Michaud has done, no harm shall come to his brothers. They are stupid, but they are Michauds." He paused as if conscious that he might have admitted too much, and then broke into a shout of shrill defiant laughter. "You Mounties! You amuse me! Yes, I have seen you parade in Regina in your little red jackets! I have seen you many times. And I have smiled to myself. Ah, yes, now you see before you Jean Michaud, gen-tle-man, schol-ar and trainer of seals. But mark my words," and his eyes flamed again, "you will never live to see Jean

Michaud stand before a judge at Aklavik. Neither will you see his brothers there. Never, I tell you . . . never!"

For a moment there was utter stillness in the igloo. And then came a low singing growl from Ruff who had resented the high pitch of Jean's voice. Jean shifted his feet nervously, looked at the ceiling and then at the small dog who had resumed his vigil of Molly's box.

"That dog!" he exclaimed angrily. "I do not like him. He is a pest with his big eyes. See! He has ruined my bag! I shall be forced to remove the tails!" and Jean held up the velvet sled bag which he had discovered and brought inside. "It is the bag in which I carried the little white balls to balance upon the seals' noses. I have said it before . . . I do not like him. Why do you have such a dog?"

CHAPTER FIFTEEN

Zack Makes a Call Upon the Michauds

AFTER breakfast the next morning, Jean's feet and hands were again freed, and he was ordered to assist Zack in harnessing the dogs. All went well until one of Jean's dogs, He-bo, jealous of Anore, attempted to take the latter's place as lead dog. Anore, wild, bad-tempered and extremely proud of his position as lead dog, sprang at He-bo, breaking loose from the harness. A bitter struggle ensued.

In the midst of the pandemonium, Jean, instead of restoring order, took advantage of the situation and ran toward the sled. Reaching between two boxes, he managed to get hold of a small brushwood hatchet which had fallen out of the utility box. Tilting the sled on one side, he was about to hack into a sled runner when Zack seized his uplifted arm. There was a sharp skirmish. Zack tripped over a rope and fell, dragging Jean with him, and together they rolled in the snow, clenched in each other's arms. Over and over they rolled, Jean still maintaining his hold on the hatchet. Then, inch by inch Zack turned him on one side, twisting his arm behind him, forcing him to release the hatchet. In the midst of the struggle Jean, realizing he was losing ground, called for Anore.

"A-nore! A-nore!" he screamed. "*Vite! Vite!*"

It was a crucial moment for Zack. Anore, loose from his harness, was free to come to Jean's aid. And should the great beast spring at him, Zack knew he would have to draw his pistol with his right hand, thereby giving Jean a chance to recover the hatchet. Moreover, if he killed Anore, there would be one less dog to pull the sled. Their traveling pace would be slackened.

But Anore, treated as a beast of burden, well fed mainly because of his imposing appearance in pulling Jean's elaborate sled, felt no great devotion for his master. There had never been affection between them. And Anore was now busily engaged in punishing He-bo. For days, He-bo had snapped and growled, greedy for first place. If Anore heard Jean's call, he paid no heed. His great jaws were reaching for He-bo's throat through a thick ruff of fur, and he had no other interest.

The hatchet, finally dropped from Jean's nerveless fingers, was kicked some distance away by Zack's foot, and the rope, so conveniently near, was used in binding Jean once more. A few moments later, Anore was forced to let go his hold of He-bo's throat because of a tight draw knot of walrus skin about his own, shutting off his breath and gagging him. He-bo, none the worse, lay panting on the snow.

"Too bad, Jean." Zack was breathing hard as he brushed the snow out of his hood. "Now you'll ride cold. The extra weight will be hard on your dogs going uphill."

"Dogs! What do I care about dogs!" screamed Jean, watching from a half-sitting position. "You, A-nore, you failed me . . . you did not come. I shall beat you!"

"It'll be a long time before you beat Anore, Jean, so save your breath. Into the bag you go!" and Zack thrust Jean inside his sleeping bag and then dragged him onto the sled.

"A copper should never let his prisoner freeze," reminded Jean.

"You'll have to do a little something for yourself from now on," returned Zack. "I'll look at your hands once in a while and you can kick your feet to keep the blood circulating. It will be chilly going but I guess you'll live through it. Remember, I warned you yesterday that this would happen if you tried to double-cross me."

Jean made no response. He had gambled and lost. Had the sled runner been destroyed, Zack would have been delayed several days. Now Jean lay inert, but his eyes were never still, squinting at the distant ridges, peering over the sides of the sled. He knew that Zack was following his brothers.

For the most part, the river was frozen, but occasionally Zack was forced to wade through shallow overflows. The trail was noticeably swinging northeast and before long they came to the spruce forest where the Michauds and Kop-a had camped the first night. It was not far off the trail, and Zack's attention was attracted to it by the marks of a sled runner which had broken through the crust as the Michauds had turned to go in. Farther on there had been another stop, as evidenced by a windbreak. Mat's unusually large feet and Kop-a's smaller ones were plainly outlined but there was no sign of Joe's. The large feet had walked back and forth between the sled and the fire several times, and Zack wondered if Joe was riding. This seemed strange in view of the fact that Joe was a vigorous person, active and hardened to the trail.

Two miles beyond they saw the second windbreak with the same pattern of footsteps. Something was wrong with the party ahead! From then on, there were many stops. Caution seemed to have been disregarded as the windbreaks remained standing, easily discernible from the river, and there were brown tobacco stains marking the snow. Meanwhile, Zack was gaining on the distance between the two parties.

It was at one of these stops that Jean broke the stillness with a perfect imitation of a wolf howl. His dogs, frightened, burst into an uproar of barking and struggled madly to free themselves from the sled. Though startled at the weird sound so near and so loud, Zack jumped and threw a heavy robe over Jean's head, muffling the warning undoubtedly meant for his brothers. The dogs were quieted, and Jean was gagged with one of his own fawnskin socks. From then on he rode helpless, his black eyes glittering and baleful, but not without a certain air of expectancy. Zack knew he was hopeful that his signal might have been heard.

In the afternoon, Ruff was to prove worthy of the affection and care which Zack and Kop-a had given him. All day long, the small dog had been uneasy. When not sleeping from exhaustion in the velvet bag, now stripped of its ermine tails, he was following at Zack's heels, excited and whimpering. Frequently he crossed the trail from side to side. And knowing that the trail was fresh, Zack saw that Ruff was aware of the nearness of the Michauds and Kop-a.

It was at the division of the main stream and one of its branches that the young policeman was forced to halt and rely upon the trailing instincts of an untrained puppy. The surfaces of the main stream and its branch were covered with water and there were no signs to indicate the passage of two sleds. Jean, silently amused at Zack's dilemma, had a scoffing light in his black eyes as Zack picked Ruff up in his arms. Even Jean's dogs seemed to wear a similar expression.

"Come on, Ruff, we've got work to do. We're going to find Kop-a, do you understand?"

Leaving Jean bound and muffled and the dogs tied to some stout willows, Zack walked down the side of the branch stream to a place where there was no overflow. Here, with the puppy close at his heels, he combed the banks for some sign of a sled mark or footprint, but to no avail. Nor was Ruff interested. He wagged his tail at the name Kop-a but most of the time stood still, gazing at Zack with mute inquiry.

"I guess it's the other river, Ruff. We'll go back."

Jean's eyes were less scornful when Zack appeared once more, carrying the small dog, and proceeded to follow the banks of the main stream. It was a quarter of a mile before they reached dry ice. Here Zack put the puppy down.

"Kop-a, Kop-a, go find Kop-a," he kept repeating. "Go find Kop-a. You did it once before . . . you can do it again. Kop-a!" True, Ruff had received one lesson in tracking but how long ago it seemed! Moreover, on that occasion he had been given a tangible clue to work with . . . the boy's mitten.

Zack led the puppy back and forth across the ice until Ruff, who had begun to sense the tenseness of the situation, broke into a wail of distress.

But Zack never lost patience. He finally seated himself on a rock to wait. Ruff ran about, dug for stones, and then wandered upstream. He was gone but a short time when Zack heard him whimper. Ruff was trailing! Little eager cries sounded in his throat as he took Zack directly to a spot where the snow had been scratched by the runners of a sled. This was all Zack needed. A little later he drove the four huskies and the sled bearing Jean straight up the main stream. And Ruff, as if conscious of his importance, led the way, a tiny black figure triumphantly waving his plumed tail.

On they climbed as the blue misty ridges became ever clearer. At last, late in the afternoon of the second day, they approached the plateau where the river widened into a shallow lake. And just as they were ascending the first steep, Zack called the dogs to a sudden halt. From the other side of the ridge had come the sound of a rifle shot.

Lakes, muskegs, black spruce, tundra . . . Concealed in low brush on the very top of a limestone ridge, Zack scrutinized the scene before him with his binoculars. He saw nothing unusual until he lifted his gaze to the second ridge. Then he drew in his breath sharply. On the side of the slope lay the dead body of a caribou with sections of meat cut away. So that was the reason for the rifle shot! The Michauds had been forced to leave most of the heavy animal; perhaps they were planning to come back for it as soon as they had made camp.

Lifting his glasses still higher, Zack gave an exclamation of surprise. There, winding their way to the top, he caught his first glimpse of the sleds ahead. As he had surmised, the Michaud sled was in the lead setting the pace, the dogs straining up the last pitch of hill. Joe was riding and Mat walked by the side of the sled to steady its weight. Fifty feet below . . . and Zack stared eagerly . . . Kop-a pushed at the back of his own sled with the Siberian runners!

The boy was alive and well! He had not suffered too severely from the scalp wound or from his icy plunge in the lake. He was obviously tired, but he was driving the dogs! Kop-a was carrying on! A surge of relief and gratitude swept over Zack. There they were . . . the boy he had come to love, and the seven dogs, from Moise at the head to Nigak, last in line. Even Barry was pulling.

As Zack watched, the sled stopped and Kop-a climbed forward to examine the moccasin on Susie's left forepaw. He was taking full responsibility, Zack told himself. Returning to the sled bars. Kop-a stumbled as if extremely weary. Just then Mat, tall and heavy in his shaggy parka, ordered him with a peremptory gesture to hurry. Already the dogs were straining in their traces. Kop-a made no effort to push them faster and there was a sign of defiance in the way he carried himself, his head high and his shoulders straight.

"Bravo, my boy," said Zack softly.

The top of the ridge was gained at last, and the dogs and the sled went over. Only Kop-a remained behind, a single figure on the skyline. He turned to scan the land back of him and Zack knew it was he for whom the boy was searching. With a sudden impulse, he stood up and waved both arms. But the distance between them was too great. Kop-a did not see him and turned away; probably Mat was calling him from below on the other side.

Once more Zack swept his glasses over the silent and empty ridge, now stained crimson by the evening sunset. Wherever he focused, the picture of Kop-a appeared before him, a slight lonely figure, every line of his body weary but undaunted, hopeful of some glimpse of him and still believing him to be alive. Zack's throat felt tight and there was a mist of anger before his eyes when he finally slipped his binoculars back into their leather case. There was a job to be done and it must be done that night.

For a long time the fire had burned brightly in the Michaud camp. Zack had first spied it from the center of the second ridge. Two tents were pitched close by. Because of the wind which circled about him and might carry his scent to the Michaud dogs as well as his own, he had been forced to swing north and then face the main wind which came from the south. For an hour or so he had lost sight of the camp as he worked his way through a forest of lichen-hung spruce. Emerging at the northern end of the ridge, he had found the Michauds' fire burning as brightly as ever. He had left

Jean some distance away, securely bound in a hastily constructed igloo, and Ruff had been leashed to a stake just inside the door. He knew that he alone must finish the job at hand that night.

But Zack was perplexed as he descended the second ridge and traveled slowly toward the Michaud camp. Why were they burning a brushwood fire so openly and without caution? It was midnight and already the fire had burned four hours. Facing the bright flames, it was difficult for him to approach unseen. And Mat had been much in evidence, walking between the fire and the first tent, lugging pails of water. Kop-a was last seen moving towards the second tent. Zack was now positive Joe was in the first tent, ill.

The night had turned cloudy; there were no stars and the wind still shifted frequently. Zack balanced himself on the lower limb of a spruce until the fire smoldered and Mat was asleep. The Michaud dogs barked almost continuously and it seemed strange to him that he could not hear sounds from any of his own dogs. Where was Nigak, who never lost the opportunity to air his voice?

Mat had been absent for half an hour and the fire had lessened when Zack decided to move forward before the wind changed again. Except for the dogs, the entire camp was still. Walking in a direct line, he could see neither dogs nor sleds in front of Kop-a's tent. He was within fifty feet of the first tent now, stepping softly, his hand on his pistol, when he heard a heavy groan. There was no mistaking Joe's deep guttural voice. Joe, the brains of the Michauds, was too ill to take charge and this explained the reason for the brightly burning fire and the lack of discretion! As Zack paused for a moment, Mat unexpectedly came out of the tent, carrying a pail. In the gray light he appeared stooped in his heavy parka, and staggered as if he had just been awakened from sleep. The dogs, who had now spied the policeman, were barking loudly. Mat yelled at them and then bent over the fire, still unaware of Zack's approach. The dogs continued their noisy barking and Mat, at last sensing some real cause for the disturbance, turned about.

"No noise, Mat! Put up your hands!"

In his surprise, Mat dropped a pail of scalding water, which hissed against the cold snow. As he held up his hands, Zack removed a pistol from his pocket.

"All right, Denny," Mat mumbled. He appeared more dazed than startled, and in the light of the fire his face seemed drawn and thin. "I don't know as I cares so much one way n'other. Joe's hurt in there."

"What happened to him?"

"That black cur-pup of the kid's bit 'im. Joe's awful sick. Thinks a bear's a-chasin' 'im. Blood poisonin'."

"Is he conscious at times?"

"I dunno. I ain't sure. 'E's full of queer notions."

"Jean's over in my camp."

"Jean's in yer camp?" Bewilderment shown in Mat's face. "So yer got Jean." He drew a long breath. "Well, I guess 'e had it comin' to 'im. So both Joe and Jean is done in." Mat's head drooped forward.

"You've all had it coming. You can't dodge the law forever, Mat."

"Wot yer arrestin' me fer, Denny?" and Mat looked up with a little of his former truculency.

"For aiding and abetting Jean. The party you sold reindeer skins to in Coldhill talked plenty after you left the last time. You and Joe must have made a pretty little pile."

"So that's it," said Mat dully. "Well," and his head sank forward despondently again, "I guess yer got us, red coat. The two of 'em has nigh ruined me. Joe a-worshipin' Jean an' Jean a-worshipin' the devil. I'm sick of it all . . . I'm tired . . . I'm wore out. I don't care wot they do ter me now. Joe's a-dyin'. Ain't you a doc, Denny? Don't they learn you medicine at yer school? We've got some of yer bottles in there," and Mat, the half-wit, nodded toward the first tent. Tears began to run down his worn cheeks and he mopped them up with his fur mitten.

"Maybe I can help. But first, I want to see the boy. Is he in the other tent?"

"The kid's gone. 'E ain't in any tent."

"What do you mean, gone? If either you or Joe touched a hair of his head . . ."

"Naw, naw, 'e runned away three hours back. Took yer dogs wit' 'im. 'E's gone ter find yer. Been crazy wi' worry. But 'e ain't got no gun an' 'e cain't go fur. 'E's gotter come back or the bears'll git 'im. I couldn't fetch 'im an' leave Joe. Joe's a-dyin' . . ." and Mat, tall and stooped like a huge ragged bear himself in the dim light, began to cry again.

Meanwhile, back in the igloo, Ruff was engaged in chewing his leash which was made of caribou thongs and not of an objectionable flavor. Suddenly finding himself free, he strutted about happily, eyeing Molly's box, while Jean, muffled and bound, watched with agonized eyes. The battle commenced. The squirrel, routed from her nest, scolded and barked her defiance but was finally forced to flee ignominiously through a crack between two blocks of snow.

Jean writhed and turned helplessly as Ruff then attacked the nest. Over the ground were strewn dry leaves, moss, small sticks, bird feathers, root bulbs and strangest of all, the ivory sheath of an old hunting knife. Ruff eyed this last item with favor . . . stones had been scarce that day. But he found it brittle between his sharp young teeth. It splintered into bits and from some pussy willow cotton inside dropped a large green button, beautifully carved, old and worn with time. The button rolled into the middle of the igloo where it settled in a small hollow of snow. Outside, Molly could be heard scolding from the top of the roof.

CHAPTER SIXTEEN

Kop-a Alone on the Trail

ESCAPE from the Michaud camp had not been difficult. Scarcely breathing lest he be heard, Kop-a made his way to the sled and securely roped the primus stove to the oil drum which was almost full. An unusually loud groan from Joe made the boy pause as he lashed down the tarpaulin over the packs and sleeping bags. But heavy breathing followed, and Kop-a then walked to where the dogs were staked.

"Quiet, Moise. Quiet, Nigak, quiet." Noiselessly, Kop-a had crept among them. Already the dogs were fond of this boy who fed and looked after them so carefully. Moise, whose heart wholly belonged to Zack, was quivering with excitement, as though he sensed they were about to go. His eyes glowed in the gray light and he ran forward eagerly to his place at the head of the team.

All was ready. "Mush, Moise," called Kop-a in a low voice. There was a slight creaking sound as the runners freed themselves from the frozen snow and slid smoothly over a light crust.

"Gee!" came the next command, and Moise obediently headed south. The cries of the Michaud dogs faded in the distance as the sled disappeared into the night, the dogs' bodies swaying, their feet moving in a pattern step.

At the bottom of the first hill, Moise, the hunter, spied an Arctic hare. With resounding yelps, the dogs bore sharply to the left in pursuit. Made hungry by the sight of red caribou meat, which they had not shared in the killing that afternoon, they caught the spirit of the chase. The sled, pulled abruptly to one side, would have turned over had not Kop-a, remembering Zack's tactics, thrown his weight to the opposite side as balance. On the dogs raced, heedless of the whip! The brake, scraping noisily along the snow, appeared useless. A turn to the right, a turn to the left . . . they wound in and out between lichen-draped spruce. The hare, which ran more like a dog than a rabbit, skimmed the surface of a hill and seemingly disappeared into the sky beyond. Gaining the top of the hill, the dogs slid down a steep incline, the sled crowding at their heels. Then abruptly, amazingly, they came to a stop on a narrow shelf of rock, Moise bracing himself as a bulwark against the entire pack.

Kop-a, frightened by the rate of speed at which they had traveled, stared stupefied before him. Perilously close loomed a dark open space. A mist hung over the abyss and far below could be heard the sound of running water. Had the sled gone down, none of them would have survived. With a shudder the boy wondered about the hare. Had it leaped to the bottom in its fright, or was it now gazing at them from the cover of some brushwood?

"Back, Moise. Back, Brindy." His hands, holding the reins, were shaking, and it seemed as if the dogs sensed this fear which gripped him. Barry whined and

Susie scolded in her excitement. Moise obeyed eagerly, glad to leave the edge of the ravine, and the rest of the dogs fell in line.

A moment later Kop-a was staring over his shoulder, remembering Mat. Had Mat heard Moise yelp when he sighted the rabbit? How glad he was now that he had left the tent in its place. Mat, lugging pails of water, would have been sure to note its absence. If Mat should discover Zack's sled and dogs were gone . . . ah, he had not thought of that!

Up the hill went the sled, as Kop-a continued to scan the crest, still fearful that Mat might appear, waving his arms. At the top, he drew a long breath . . . Mat was not in sight. Trees screened with lichen lined the way. Several times, he thought they were Mat. With his eyes on the trees and the next two bends, he let the dogs take the lead. On he went, past the granite boulder, which he was sure he remembered, watching always for Mat. Would Mat shoot in order to stop him? No, Mat had not come. He had not left Joe.

Suddenly Kop-a pulled the dogs to a stop. He had a vague recollection of having passed a thicket of willows as the dogs raced after the hare. A branch had scratched his cheek. But where were the willows now?

Back and forth he searched while the dogs waited. The snow lay level and unmarked before him and in the gray light there were no traces of a sled's runners. Kneeling, he felt with his bare hands for some indentation in the snow. Engrossed in watching for Mat, he had assumed the dogs would follow their own trail back. He had seen them do it before. It had seemed simple enough . . . a turn to the left, a turn to the right and then another turn to the right . . . or was it left? Suddenly he remembered having heard that sometimes tired dogs traveled with the wind rather than take its buffeting. And these dogs were tired . . . they had pulled steadily for two days. Perhaps he had expected too much from them. Carefully Kop-a retraced his steps back to the boulder. And then he noticed that a single trail marked the snow. It was not the same boulder he had passed in the beginning!

Dismayed and perplexed, he gazed about him. The snow in all directions lay unmarred, unscratched. And all the trees appeared the same, the wind softly singing through the swaying lichen. The sky seemed to have shut down upon him in a smothering gray, and for the first time Kop-a felt a sense of helplessness. He knew now that he could not trust the dogs for direction. Let a hare cross their path and they became maddened creatures. The narrow escape from the abyss had left him shaken. Would there be other black ravines yawning ahead? Where was he now on the map which Zack and he had studied in Sandy McArdle's cabin?

A wind still blew and unless its direction had shifted, it came from the south. Facing it for an hour or so and then swinging to the right would bring him to the second ridge. E. B. had said if ever Zack and he became separated on the tundra, to go north and avoid traveling in circles. In that way they would meet somewhere on the coast. But he was not free to go north. Over to the west beyond two ridges, Zack, on foot, was struggling with cold and hunger. There was no other choice.

Suddenly conscious that the dogs were watching him, Kop-a looked up. From white-faced Moise to little Susie, they stood motionless and silent, as if waiting for him to come to a decision. Zack's dogs . . . raised by him from puppyhood . . . knowing no other master! Even the sled with its familiar hoop handle and Siberian runners stood dimly outlined, ready to go. . . .

"Mush, Moise! Gee! Gee!" The dogs leaned in their collars, and again they faced the wind from the south.

A few hours later, Lingo's harness gave way. Kop-a was at a loss how to mend it until a search through Zack's emergency box brought forth a rusty nail and some thongs. With numbed fingers he bored holes through the rawhide harness and tied the broken ends together. The dogs stood with lowered heads as he worked, their bodies sagging with weariness. Another Arctic hare scampered by, but this time they took no notice. With sudden decision, the boy unharnessed and staked the dogs, giving each one the additional fish he had not received for his supper. The supply of fish was even lower than he had reckoned and he planned to cook them meal and tallow at his first opportunity. He himself was not hungry, and had traveled along tirelessly, buoyed with excitement at being free once more.

The sky was still gray above, with no stars visible. For his camp Kop-a chose a secluded spot behind a clump of willows. With a wall of snow blocks and the sled pulled close to form a V, he felt that he would have protection enough for one night.

After finding a snow knife, he set to work to cut the

blocks. The first snow was too soft; the blocks crumbled in his arms. Walking in another direction, he found snow of a firmer consistency. The blocks made a peculiar squeaking noise as he fitted them together. Spruce, covered with the bear rug, made a warm foundation for his sleeping bag. Already the dogs were asleep, except Moise, whose eyes were only half-closed and whose ears lifted at every sound.

"Moise," Kop-a said softly, walking close to the lead dog and putting out his hand a little timidly. Moise was not like the other dogs and Kop-a had never felt at ease with this white husky who loved to hunt and was so devoted to Zack. But he longed for some recognition of the dog's support in that hour. Moise did not offer to touch the extended hand but looked up at him out of eyes very dark in his white face. He seemed to be steeling himself lest the hand pet him, but he did not growl.

"We're on our way to find Zack," said Kop-a, feeling as though he were addressing a person. The dog continued to look at him but did not stir. As Kop-a turned away, however, he thought he saw the white bushy tail move. Of all the dogs, he needed Moise as a friend. Perhaps in a little time . . .

Removing his arteegee and parka, Kop-a crawled into his sleeping bag. And almost immediately, his body curled close to the walls of his shelter, he was asleep.

Geese crying hoarsely overhead and the warm sun beating down finally awakened him. On top of his sleeping bag was new snow which had fallen lightly during the night. Startled and dismayed, he sat upright. The snow was just deep enough to hide yesterday's trail made by the Michauds over the ridge. He had seen Zack dig beneath to find an old trail, but this was an accomplishment which came of training and experience. He looked over the walls of his shelter to see if his own tracks, made only a few hours earlier, were visible. The surface was smooth, leveled by the wind except for the rounded backs of the seven sleeping dogs.

In his plans for escape, he had considered his lack of tent, compass, gun and supplies. They were the hazards which haunted him the two days he had been forced to follow the Michauds. He had weighed and measured his assets and liabilities until he knew them by heart. It had been impossible to bring the tent. As to the compass, Zack had undoubtedly taken it with him. And Mat and Joe had most of Zack's supplies. The sun, the north star, the birds flying northward, and any of the landmarks he could remember, would have to be his compass. All would be well when he met Zack. Together they would find Ruff. And they would not starve, for there was snaring wire packed on the sled and Zack would still be carrying his two service pistols.

But the weather . . . he had given little thought to the weather. Now a new fear gripped him. What would he do in case of a squall? He had witnessed the fury of one on the shores of Ivory Horn. The force and scream of the wind had been terrifying. What would he do alone, without a shelter?

There was no answer to this last question. Kop-a arose and put on his parka and arteegee. His throat felt choked as he breakfasted meagerly on caribou liver and tea. He had been eager, so eager to make his escape. And now the full seriousness of his handicaps began to dawn on him. This was the land of the wolf and grizzly bear. Wolves were afraid of fire and fortunately his matches were dry in their metal box. As for bear . . . he had always wanted to kill a grizzly, but in that hour the thought of an encounter sent him into a panic.

There was nothing left, no other choice than to make his own trail over the two ridges. Perhaps from the higher ridge, crossed only yesterday, he would be able to see the lake in the distance. On the other hand, Mat and Joe's trail had swung northeast and the lake might not be in sight. His bearings were solely dependent upon seeing the lake, and if the lake was not there . . . The thought left him chilled and heavy. His hands were cold and perspiring within his mittens and he realized he was frightened. If the lake was not there, he would be forced to hurry north . . . without Zack.

After breakfast, the dogs were harnessed and they were on their way, heading west toward the ridge which rose in the distance. Great pools of water lay on the wide stretches of snow, and as Kop-a drew nearer he saw that they were small lakes, partially melted, bordered by wisps of dried sedge grass. The geese, still crying, circled about them, possibly remembering them as former nesting places.

With a rifle, he might have managed to kill a few . . . enough for one meal. He wondered if it would be possible to reach one with the long-handled chisel knife given to Zack by E. B. as a parting gift. It was worth trying, he thought, and unstrapped it from the sled. The birds had lighted on the water, beautiful creatures with brownish-gray bodies, black heads and necks, with white cheek patches. When they flew, there were broad white stripes across the upper parts of their wings. For a while, he tried creeping up to them as they swam close to the edge of the water, but each bird took flight whenever he raised an arm to take aim. Finally they left in a body for a lake beyond. Again that futile helpless feeling came over him . . . another undertaking had failed.

The sun seemed unusually bright that noon. Kop-a found that he was squinting and that there were tears on his cheeks. Zack's amber snow glasses gave immediate relief. All that morning the sled wove in and out between the small lakes. The flying geese always seemed to be just a bit ahead but now their cries were company for him, breaking the stillness of the surrounding country. Early in the afternoon, he stopped for jerky and tea at the foot of the ridge. Here he decided to cross, forging his own way.

"Haw, Moise!"

The dogs pulled willingly up the steep slope but soon became exhausted. Brindy groaned audibly, Susie scolded, and Barry stood still at times, refusing to move. He laid his plump body down to rest and no amount of prodding could stir him until he was ready. The suspense of waiting, of hoping to see the lake from the top was almost more than Kop-a could endure.

On they climbed . . . slipping, hauling, pushing . . .

and at last they reached their goal. Panting heavily, perspiring, the boy wiped the steam from his glasses and looked ahead. Across stretched another ridge and beyond that . . . land. But it was white . . . white . . . all white. There was not a single dark line of trees to denote the shore of any lake. Tundra, miles of tundra . . . He was still far north of any familiar landmark.

Had he traveled east instead of west after leaving the ravine? The very thought so appalled him that he sat down on the edge of the sled, his knees weak. Only the sound of a whimper from one of the dogs broke the silence, for the geese had gone and there was no sign of life on the small lakes below. Rather than face the dog's questioning eyes, he leaned forward, his head resting on his arms. He had failed . . . failed miserably. Everything he had attempted had failed . . . From the moment Moise had sighted the scurrying hare, his plans had miscarried. . . .

The sun had been gone for the last hour or so, and a grayness settled down upon them once more. Kop-a did not know which way to turn unless it was to follow the geese flying northward. And they had long since gone. Somehow, he must find Lucas. Lucas would return with him and search for Zack, if it was not too late. . . . He was finally roused by the touch of Barry's warm tongue against his cheek.

CHAPTER SEVENTEEN

Bear!

LATE that afternoon Kop-a sighted the rounded sides of an igloo in the distance. Excited, forgetting his weariness, he raced the dogs forward until he realized the house was quite far away. As he came nearer, he saw to his great disappointment that it was empty. No smoke came from the hole in the roof and no one came running to meet him. Built of stout willows, driftwood and sod, it had apparently been deserted for some time.

The boy entered and gazed about him. The day's exceptionally warm sun had partially melted the snow on the roof and a pool of water had formed on the decayed driftwood floor. Rusty cans, a child's bone top, castoff skins, and rags lay scattered about. But it was a shelter and he unloaded, taking inside every article he could carry. A shed at the rear housed the dogs.

By night he was fairly well established, relieved to have a covering overhead. The pool of water was again frozen, the heavy bear robe hung at the door, and the sled tarpaulin was tied to the roof with thongs to cover the holes where the sod had given way. As he was about to prepare the dogs' mash, measuring the meal into Zack's largest kettle, his eye caught sight of a line of white which had formed under the curtain at the door. Snow! He had found this shelter none too soon!

Great flakes were falling outside and there was a humming sound in the distance which grew into a roar as he listened. It was like the muttering of angry voices coming nearer, growing louder. Within a few moments the storm was raging, clamoring across the tundra toward the mountains in the east. All that night and the next day the air was white with swirling flakes, mounting in deep banks at one side of the igloo. The small shed housing the dogs completely disappeared.

In order to forget the storm outside as much as possible, Kop-a tried several diversions. One was to bake bannock for his supper. The cake scorched, filling the igloo with smoke, but he ate it, washing it down with tea. Afterwards, he played the victrola. Unfortunately, he selected one of Zack's favorite records, and the familiar strains of music, thin and piping in contrast to the roar of the wind, sent the dogs into a panic of barking and himself into gloomy speculation. Was Zack out in this storm? Had he found Ruff and, together, were they trying to follow the trail of the two sleds? Rousing himself, he warmed some water and bathed and rebound his head, after washing and drying the gauze. The gauze dried in a stringy fashion and it was difficult to use Zack's method of bandaging. In every thing Kop-a attempted he found himself simulating Zack, from the building of windbreaks on the trail, the driving of dogs, the loading and unloading of the sled, to the baking of bannock. His few days of travel with the policeman had taught him much. His first attempts were not always successful but he persevered and invariably profited by the experience.

Tired and depressed, Kop-a finally fell asleep and awakened late the next morning to find the storm still raging. For breakfast he ate sparingly of the last can of beans and drank a great deal of hot tea. Then with a hatchet he chopped a small hole in the sod and willow, making a passageway between the igloo and the dogs' shed. A little later, crawling on his hands and knees, his begrimed face and bandaged head greeted the joyful dogs through the opening.

Throughout the early afternoon he slept. Later he cut circles of caribou skin and made moccasins for the dogs' feet. As he worked he allowed them, one by one, to come into the igloo with him for company, blocking the passageway with heavy packs until each dog had finished his call. All went well until Barry's turn came. Having enjoyed himself hugely, his mouth curled in its accustomed grin, the big gray puppy was loath to depart and had to be shoved back to his quarters by main force through the small opening. In his resisting state, Barry seemed to expand and for a while Kop-a believed he would have to enlarge the door. A final heave, however, shot the puppy through with unbelievable speed, much to Kop-a's relief and Barry's disappointment.

And then came Moise's turn. The lead dog, his dark eyes alert, was not at ease. Avoiding Kop-a, he walked about in a caged fashion, his whole body tense, and at length settled down close to the wall. For a long while he remained motionless, and finally slept, his great white head on his paws. And because he seemed content, Kop-a left him there for the night, glad of his company.

With dawn came the sun. As though from a great distance, came the barking of many dogs. Kop-a, dreaming that he heard once more Ruff's agonized cries when he was deserted at Ivory Horn, finally became conscious of the deafening din as coming from the dogs in the shed. They were answering a high wail in the distance. Could it be Moise's call? Had Moise become loose? Now fully awakened, he sat up abruptly and looked about the igloo. Cold air blew against his face. The bear rug hung by one corner to the driftwood door frame. Moise had gone!

New snow lay piled in sharp-edged drifts some two hundred feet away. Thigh-deep in these drifts loomed the dark figure of a large brown bear! Standing at bay, upright on his hind legs, the bear faced Moise just beyond his reach. A steel trap with a broken chain swung at one end of a heavy forepaw.

One lone dog against a grizzly! Moise, the intrepid! Moise the hunter, his courage greater than his wisdom! Stalled by the impeding drifts, the bear filled the air with roars of anger, frequently shaking the trap violently as if to be rid of it. His long shoulder hair stood stiffly on end. Above all could be heard Moise's call for the other dogs.

Frantic in his haste, Kop-a stumbled among the boxes and cooking pans until he reached the small doorway he had made the day before. Pulling away the heavy packs, he let the excited dogs stream out, one after the other, yelping shrilly. Through the igloo they raced, across windswept spaces to the drifts, King and Nigak in the lead. Last to come through was Barry.

Less daring than Moise, the seven dogs halted cautiously at a certain distance from the bear who snarled ferociously at his new opponents and swung his head from side to side as if seeking a way of escape. Now and then he gulped snow to relieve his thirst, but he kept his small angry eyes ever upon the waiting dogs. Then slowly, feeling his way and growling the while, the grizzly began to back his way out of the drifts. The dogs followed step by step.

It was then that Moise leaped at the bear's throat. With scarcely a moment's hesitation, the other dogs closed in on all sides. The air was filled with flying snow, howls, snarls and barking. Caught by one of the bear's forepaws, Moise was sent through the air at terrific speed. The dog landed on his head but bounded up instantly and was back with the others, apparently none the worse for his punishment. Susie, small and quick, concentrated her efforts at the rear of the bear. Her sharp teeth must have had a telling effect through his thick hide, for once his body rose into the air with a yell of rage. Susie screamed excitedly as she barely missed the lightning pass of the big paw which descended in her direction. But faithful to her cohorts, she remained at her post. And each time the bear struck at her, the other dogs attacked, playing their parts like a rehearsed chorus.

Meanwhile Kop-a, a horrified spectator, watched from the doorway of the igloo, helpless to assist in any way, only too conscious of his need of a gun. How was this great brown beast to be killed? Could the dogs eventually overpower it? It seemed impossible. Time after time, Moise was hurled back by the bear's mighty fore paw, and each time the boy sickened at the sight. The dog was limping and dragging a hind foot. King was bleeding at the mouth. Barry, underfoot most of the time, now crouched at the side lines, having received rough treatment from the onrushing dogs as well as from the bear. And slowly, surely, the grizzly was backing toward the igloo, intent upon using it as a vantage point. Kop-a knew he must look about for a means of defense. His only possible weapons were the snow knife, the hatchet and the long-handled chisel knife. The chisel knife had failed him once, in his attempt to reach the birds. But he chose it now, slipped on his parka, and went outside.

Ever nearer came the bear, swinging the trap in a frenzied manner and moving his head from side to side. Moise was obviously weakening, and Lingo had been sent spinning through the air for a distance of twenty feet. Kop-a knew he must act quickly before the dogs became disabled. If only he could climb to the top of the igloo, he might make a surprise attack upon the grizzly as he stood below. Would the sod and willows hold his weight?

He chose a place where the snow was shallow and with the aid of the chisel's long handle, propped himself and mounted, feeling through the snow with his mittened hand for something to hold to. The sod was loose in places. Cautiously he felt his way, clinging to the ice chisel with one hand, steadying himself when necessary, and hanging to any available branch of willow within reach. Gradually he went higher, his feet forcing their way for toe holds, his hand groping in the snow. All sorts of fearful possibilities ran through his mind. If the willow gave way, it might send him crashing below into the igloo at about the time the bear came through the door. Also, if he did not reach his position over the door soon enough, he would lose his chance of spearing the animal in the open. But the most difficult task lay ahead . . . not to lose his balance on the sloping roof at the crucial moment and fall among the fighting dogs and grizzly!

Testing each step carefully, Kop-a crawled forward. From his precarious position near the top he could see Brindy and Nigak as they leaped back and forth, and he knew the bear must be close by. Then came the delicate task of lowering himself to a spot directly over the door. Holding fast to a branch of the willow, he felt with his feet for some solid brace. Lower, lower . . . once he slipped and his heart seemed to leap into his mouth, but he drove the knife into the roof for support. This gave him a new idea and from then on he jabbed the blade into the frozen turf for balance. Gradually, slowly, inch by inch and holding his breath in suspense, he lowered his body until he reached the end of the slope and his right foot found security in the crotch of two branches. A cry of joy escaped him, so great was his relief. Fortunately it was drowned in the hubbub of noise below. Catching his breath and holding firmly to a willow root with one hand, he leaned over.

In the excitement of the fight, he had not been discovered. The bear, sitting on his haunches, was directly beneath, swinging and banging the trap against the walls of the igloo with terrific force. The lowered head, the maned hump on the back, and the white-tipped shaggy fur on the upper part of his body could easily be seen now. But most harrowing of all to Kop-a were the long curved claws on the heavily furred forearms. Every fibre within him recoiled. He had seen such claws before on the carcasses of dead bears, but never so menacing, never so alive and so near!

A dull thud and a scream of pain from Susie aroused Kop-a. Zack's dogs, if not soon relieved, would be at the mercy of those claws! His own life would be at stake. He must act as he had planned, for in a little while it might be too late. If he failed . . . but he must not fail! Steadying himself with his left hand, he bent forward. A film of mist seemed to come before his eyes. He waited until it cleared and then with all his might drove the sharp-edged ice chisel at the head of the bear. It struck, slipped and glanced off at one side! With a roar of pain and surprise, the grizzly looked up at him, his mouth wide open, showing its red interior and white fangs. In another moment, the big brown body turned toward him. A fore paw, with the long claws extended, was reaching for his foot!

Almost numb with terror, Kop-a lunged the second time. The knife struck, slipped, and then sank deep between the eyes of the uplifted face just as Moise and King attacked from either side and bore the animal backward. With one concentrated leap, the other dogs sprang, a mass of twisting, snarling beasts!

Faint, nauseated, his head reeling, the boy was forced to let go of the ice chisel and cling with both hands to the willow root. The chisel, his only weapon of defense, fell to the snow below. Summoning all his remaining strength and courage, he turned and looked down. The bear had risen and was lurching back in the direction of the drifts once more. Blood streamed from the wound in his head, blinding his eyes, and both paws swung wildly at the still pursuing dogs. And then, as Kop-a watched, the brown grizzly stopped. There was a gasping gurgle, a soft swishing sound as the big body rolled over in the snow, the dogs on top. The ice chisel had done its work!

Kop-a half fell, half jumped from the roof of the igloo to the ground below. His knees failed to support him as he landed and he sprawled lengthwise. Lifting his head, he gazed about him. The dogs were swarming around the bear, barking with excitement and triumph. All but Moise, who lay at one side, his white fur streaked with blood.

CHAPTER EIGHTEEN

On the Tundra

MOISE was dragged on a deerskin mat into the igloo. He made no sound as he looked up at Kop-a out of pain-glazed eyes. After the other dogs had been safely housed in the shed, the boy warmed water and bathed Moise's blood-stained fur, never attempting to bind the wounds for he knew the dog himself would take care of them later. In a short time, Moise began to move about, much to Kop-a's relief.

The other dogs had not been seriously injured. King's face had been cut and torn by the bear's claws. Nigak had a gash on his flank. Susie had apparently received a spanking for she sat herself down with great care and generally preferred to remain standing. With the exception of Moise, they had come through the experience with little damage. And because of Moise's condition, Kop-a decided to wait over one day.

The arrival of the bear had been providential. The dogs' fish was gone, the mash low, and Kop-a's own supplies were dwindling. The meat of the bear would give all of them strength to go ahead. But it was with some reluctance that Kop-a set about skinning the bear. How easily Lucas and Sol had skinned their game, their strong brown hands cutting the tissue with sharp knives, rolling back the hide, carefully peeling it off the paws!

He tried to remember every detail as he had seen it done. Already his bear was growing stiff as it lay on its back in the snow.

With one of Zack's sharpest knives, he made a mid-line incision through the skin from the neck to the lowest point of the abdomen. The hide was tough, the fur heavy and coarse. Then he ran the knife down the inside of each hind leg and forearm in lines as straight as possible, rolling the skin back from these parts. It was necessary to use the small blade of his own jackknife on a fore paw. The skin finally peeled off like a glove and there remained a structure so closely resembling the human hand that the boy paused, repulsed. He remembered feeling a similar aversion upon seeing the undressed paws of Lucas' and Sol's bears! His stomach feeling none too steady, he decided to cut the bone at the wrist and ankles and leave them unskinned. And to avoid disfiguring the delicate tissue about the ears, nose and mouth, he severed the spine at the neck with the hatchet, leaving the head whole and still attached to the hide. After removing the hide, with the three feet and head still undressed, he rolled the entire pelt as tightly as possible and lashed it to the side of the sled, along with the trap. By the time he had finished, the afternoon had slipped away. The pink, firm meat provided the dogs and himself with a good supper that night, and a large portion was packed on the sled for the journey ahead.

Bright, clear weather followed the storm. For the next five days Kop-a traveled across the tundra. It was not easy to lift Moise, his hind legs limp and useless, to the top of the sled each morning. It became an ordeal which both he and the dog dreaded. Though Moise tried to help, the brunt of his weight fell upon Kop-a. But once perched in his high position upon the load which was covered with the tarpaulin, the big white dog made an imposing sight. He accepted his role as passenger with dignity, staring into the distance beyond and now and then shifting the position of his sore body to ease its pain. But through it all, he remained aloof and separate.

Kop-a found deserted igloos to sleep in the first two nights, and he pulled Moise inside with him on the deerskin rug. The third and fourth nights they slept in the open behind windbreaks of snow. A squall struck them suddenly one afternoon from the northwest. The wind blew furiously for a few moments as he lay clinging to the sled, but the sun quickly melted the thin film of snow which had powdered him and the huddled dogs. Hardly able to believe his good fortune in escaping so easily, the boy struggled to his feet and hurried on, gauging his direction always by the flying birds, the sun by day, and the north star by night.

He allowed little time for sleep. The dogs, fed generously now, stood up well to their tasks, in spite of their weariness. But the strain was telling upon Kop-a . . . the strain of not knowing his whereabouts, the fear of squalls, the long hours of trekking and the stringent diet of bear meat and tea. The horror of being forced to cross a lake or river penetrated even his dreams. He had not been able to forget his plunge into the icy waters of Ivory Horn and any ice, lake or river, was unsafe now. For the sun was climbing higher in the heavens and spring was close upon them. Snow melted each noon and filled little hollows with black water. Grass began to show in wide patches. Overhead, the white-fronted goose, the black brant and the squaw duck soared northward, their harsh screams cutting the silence.

One day Kop-a imagined that he had come across his own sled tracks. For a moment he stood rigid with suspense, fearful that he had been traveling in circles! But the marks proved to be a freakish prank of the wind, which etched strange patterns on the snow. To make sure there could be no mistake, he knelt and measured; to his great relief, he found the width between his runners wider than the space between the marks.

Once he reached the coast, there would be a well-traversed trail of high brown cliffs to guide him. Eskimos, hunters, and traders would be following the same trail. Again he would be in touch with human beings and hear the sound of voices. He would quickly reach Lucas and then they would turn back for Zack. Would it be too late? It was better not to think about Zack and to march stolidly ahead. Four long tortuous days . . . four short nights . . . Must the sky always meet the tundra in that even white line? Would there never be a break in those wide flat plains?

On the morning of the fifth day Kop-a overslept. He was finally awakened by the warmth of the sun on his cheek, and he turned restlessly, dreading to rise. Then suddenly, almost in his ear, there was a brittle snapping noise. All his senses alert now, he sat up and looked about him.

Barry lay staked close by, tearing at something which he held between his two big fore paws, a look of sublime contentment on his face. Kop-a shaded his eyes and looked more carefully. From the side of the puppy's mouth hung one of the bows of Zack's amber-colored snow glasses which he had been wearing! He had tucked them under his sleeping bag but somehow they had worked their way outside and blown with the wind in Barry's direction. With a loud whoop, which startled the rest of the sleeping dogs, Kop-a scrambled out of his bag and grabbed the glasses from the surprised puppy. Hastily he examined them. One of the bows had been ripped away and the other loosened, but the glass itself was intact. Snowblindness! Without the amber glasses, he would soon have become blind facing the steady glare of the spring sun upon the snow. It would be the worst of all afflictions to endure. These shocks of near disaster were stealing his courage, wearing him down. With a piece of string, he managed to tie the glasses on beneath his woolen cap.

That afternoon he allowed himself the luxury of riding upon the sled for a little while. His mukluks were getting thin and his feet were sore. But he never allowed himself the privilege again. For without realizing it, he fell asleep leaning against the bearskin, waking up some time later to find the dogs standing still, headed in the wrong direction. According to his watch, they had lost a good hour. And in spite of all he could do after that, he could not make the dogs hurry. Their feet, as well as his, seemed to be weighted.

Occasionally sky and tundra reeled together. Alarmed,

Kop-a stopped and made tea, remembering how careful Zack was to keep himself fit. He even decided to make a stew for supper that night, and when they should finally rest he planned to drink the last of the chocolate milk before going to sleep. After that . . . He did not dare to think . . . Surely, they must be drawing nearer to the coast.

Late in the afternoon he thought he saw a hill in the distance. But he was becoming accustomed to mirages on the tundra. They beckoned and promised with misleading hope. In one moment, a settlement of igloos would loom ahead and a moment later, discouraged and disillusioned, he would be gazing once more at the flat desert of snow. Banks of mist formed strange shapes, built weird cities. He determined not to believe what he saw but to travel with his head downward, fortifying himself against that moment when he would look up and find the hill gone. But as he walked along, he found his hopes mounting, his thoughts ever returning to what might be ahead. Zack's maps had shown ridges a short distance in from the coast. He had marked them with pencil, saying at the time that once they reached those heights they would be close to the sea. Was he at last approaching one of those ridges? Would this perhaps be the hour to mark the turning point?

Steeling himself, Kop-a raised his eyes. The ridge was there! Higher, nearer, it rose into the sky. New land ahead! A new height from which to look! It would be a joy to climb those steep sides, to be away from this monotonous sea of tundra. And tomorrow or the next day he might even glimpse the ocean!

"Mush, dogs, mush!"

The dogs, sensing the excitement in his voice, picked up their feet and spurted forward. Moise shifted his position and lifted his head as if smelling new and strange things. On they hurried, Kop-a clinging to the handle bar, his eyes focused on the fresh landmark, his mind dazed with fatigue.

In his hurry, he did not stop that night for supper. Every moment counted. The ridge seemed to be a haven of refuge, of safety . . . the promise that he was near the end of his journey. Once within its shadow, he would lie down and rest.

The wall of land ahead was barren of any green. Here and there patches of dry grass showed through the snow. In back of Kop-a the setting sun rimmed the clouds with fire. Rays, like ribbons of lavender, blue, lemon-yellow and soft pink, lay upon the white slope. Even in his haste, the boy's eyes caught at the beauty before him. And always the question persisted . . . would he climb the ridge that night? Could he possibly wait until the next morning? As he drew nearer, he knew he would never be content to wait. If necessary, he would drag himself to the top with his last ounce of strength.

At the bottom of the slope Kop-a rested. But feverish energy soon drove him to his feet and in a short time he was among the dogs, patting each drooping head, calling each dog by name.

"Good old King! You've done a great job. Yes, Susie, I know you're tired. Just a little further, Lingo. Come on, Barry, up! One more pull . . . I'm going home, dogs, I'm going home!" Tears of excitement coursed down his cheeks as he talked.

The tired dogs went forward. Staggering, sometimes falling, Kop-a followed close behind, pushing when he could at the handle bars. Moise clung with his paws for balance, his body flat on the tarpaulin. For once the wind was with them, helping, not hindering. It braced them, propped them forward, and parted the thick hair on Moise's back like a comb. . . .

Three times they stopped to rest. The dogs crouched to hold the sled, and Kop-a lay prone on the snow, his head buried in his arms. There was no sound but their heavy breathing. Then the team gave a final spurt, and the sled went to the top like something alive. The dogs stood waiting as the boy caught up with them, eager for his first view. Breathing heavily, he lifted his head and gazed about. A gasp of surprise shook him and his hand dropped the whip he was carrying.

Another ridge stretched some distance ahead. Its white slope was dark with the moving bodies of gray-brown animals . . . reindeer! Some were browsing, kicking away the snow with their forefeet in order to find the moss beneath. Others were lying down for the night, their crooked antlers silhouetted against the skyline like the shifting branches of small barren trees. Faint cries of "Khow! Khow!" sounded in the distance as young fawns sought their mothers. All this Kop-a seemed to take in with one glance and then his eyes dropped to the valley below where a substantial igloo built of sod and willows stood beside a frozen stream. Smoke was blowing from a narrow funnel in the roof. And from behind the igloo came a man with a gun over his shoulder.

The sudden realization that he had found companionship at last left Kop-a speechless. Before he could cry out, King and Nigak broke into a frenzy of barking. The man stopped and looked up. There was a friendly wave of his arm as he came forward, running swiftly to meet them, a Lapp dog by his side.

There was something strangely familiar in the short thickset body, the broad shoulders, the agility with which the man approached. Kop-a ran a little way and then stumbled. The ridge beyond tilted and whirled, snow felt cold against his face, and the sunset faded into nothingness. A few moments later, strong arms lifted and bore him to the igloo in the valley. The Lapp dog ran ahead and the other dogs followed quietly, their heads low with weariness.

The smell of cooking meat, the glare of an oil lamp's flame in his eyes . . . Kop-a kept his eyes closed, for he was still half dreaming that it was Lucas who had come running to meet him. He had even felt the strength of Lucas' arms about him. And now to complete the dream, he heard In-a-loo's soft voice say, "Kop-a, Kop-a, Kop-a-noo," over and over again. As the voice became louder and nearer, he decided to open his eyes.

The oil lamp had been moved to the other side of the room. Kop-a was lying in a bunk between warm skins, and a man and a woman stood nearby. Timidly he reached out a hand and felt of the man's fawnskin sleeve. The skin was soft between his fingers. No, he was not dreaming . . . it was Lucas! Kind, dark eyes, wide apart, with the familiar laugh wrinkles at the corners, looked into his own. The short black hair, the generous mouth with the scar on the chin where an ugly steer had once struck him . . . Lucas! And it was In-a-loo beside him, wearing a bright flowered cotton dress. She was holding a cup of broth and he could see the faint wisps of steam rising in the air against the light.

"I don't understand," he said thickly and forced himself to sit up. "Did I reach the coast?"

"This is the new fawning range," answered Lucas' deep voice. "We are ten miles from the coast. Now take it slowly . . ." and the cup of warm broth was held to his lips. He drank and the seasoned broth flowed into him like new life. In-a-loo's broth . . . only In-a-loo made broth like that. Nothing would ever taste so good again! He swallowed every drop and looked up into In-a-loo's face with a smile.

Then suddenly he remembered. The reason for his great haste, the strain of those endless days on the tundra, now swept over him. Only Zack counted now . . .

"Zack!" he cried. "Zack's out there! He was lost in a storm. He was on his way to get the rustlers . . . to help you, Lucas! We've got to go back and find him. We must go right now, Lucas!"

Both Lucas and In-a-loo stared at him in stunned silence. Lucas was the first to speak. "Zack?" he asked. "Zack is where?"

"Down by Ivory Horn. There was an awful storm

and he didn't come back. I tried to find him . . ." In spite of himself, his voice broke and he sagged forward as if unable to sit up any longer.

"There, there, lamb," and In-a-loo bent over him, forgetting he had outgrown such names. "You must rest, you must sleep." She pushed him back gently onto the pillows. "We will take care of everything. The dogs . . ."

"The dogs . . ." Kop-a struggled to sit up again, "they're Zack's dogs. The white one is sick. He must come inside, Lucas."

"I'll bring him in," answered Lucas. "And now do what In-a-loo says. Just answer one question if you can, Kop-a. How long ago did this happen? How many days since you saw Zack?" Lucas' face was anxious.

"A long while ago . . . I can't remember . . . It's strange but I can't remember. I . . . I've come home, Lucas." The warm broth, the comfortable bed, his great weariness were now too much. The need for sleep was like a drug, pulling at him.

"Don't worry." The words sounded far away. "We will find him . . . we will find him. . . ." Lucas' voice followed like a song as Kop-a slipped into the waiting shadows.

CHAPTER NINETEEN

A Corporal Tells His Story

THE dog is uneasy," said Lucas on the following morning.

All night long Moise had twisted and turned on his mat of deerskin, refusing to eat the bits of meat offered him, sleeping fitfully, his ears twitching at the slightest sound. In-a-loo and Lucas were now at breakfast, seated at a little short-legged table. Fumes of coffee and freshly baked bread filled the igloo and a ptarmigan stew simmered on the flat iron sheet stove.

They had scarcely slept through the night, waking from short naps to ask each other questions and exclaiming over and over in their surprise at seeing Kop-a. In-a-loo rejoiced and wept alternately over the words, "I've come home, Lucas." Happy to see the white boy she had loved and cherished in other years, sorrowing that he must later hear of their misfortunes . . . faithful In-a-loo! But he had come home! The white boy had come home! He was taller and thinner. The parka she had sent him for Christmas was stained with blood, his birthday mukluks worn thin. There were streaks on his cheeks where tears had coursed their way and a ragged bandage was on his head. Only a few years ago he had been a little boy, clinging to her at their final parting. And now he was a man!

Lucas marveled that he had traveled across the tundra alone. Why, Kop-a had never been on a long trek. He had always come and gone by water. Yes, he and Sol had let the boy drive their dogs occasionally, but never alone. And Zack's dogs, with the exception of the large white one, were in excellent condition. Their feet were not cut and they had been well fed. But to come across the tundra!

Lucas stared wonderingly at the sleeping boy. How had he managed to meet Zack? And why had he come at all? What would Mr. Paul say? Had someone written of their many misfortunes? He himself had refrained, knowing that the boy was unhappy enough as it was . . . A little later, Kop-a would waken and talk. But now they must let him sleep. Dirty and tired, still a boy to Lucas, he lay snugly curled under the spotted squirrel robe, one hand under his cheek.

More than once Lucas shook his head despondently at the possibility of finding Zack. For he himself had experienced squalls in the Lost Lands and knew that no person could withstand their cold fury without a shelter of some sort. He regretted with all his heart that he had written his friend to come. It had been too much to ask.

Between naps, Lucas cleaned his gun, mended his harness, packed supplies, and gave directions to In-a-loo about the care of the herds. Both had agreed Kop-a was in no condition to take another long trip. Lucas had decided to go himself to the Lost Lands and as soon as the boy awakened, he would start. As it was fawning season, he could not take one of the herd boys. Surely

Mr. Paul would not object to the venture if he knew of it.

And so the night wore away. The sun rose and climbed high while Kop-a, still dressed in his flannel shirt and heavy trousers, slept on, his breathing slow and regular. Toward the end of breakfast, Moise had raised himself and given a short cry. Lucas put down his coffee cup and moved to the door.

"That dog can hear things miles away," he said.

"Moise," called a voice from the bunk. The dog turned his head and looked at the boy pleadingly. Kop-a, half stupefied with sleep, was sitting up, rubbing his eyes.

"He wants me to find Zack," said Kop-a, as if talking to himself. "It's you, isn't it, Lucas?" he asked, squinting his eyes. Through a haze, both In-a-loo and Lucas were smiling at him. The sun streamed through a window and two loaves of bread stood cooling at the back of the stove. His parka, brushed and cleaned, hung by the door. "How long have I slept?"

Before anyone could answer, Moise cried again and began to drag himself toward the door. Kop-a stood up, swaying as he reached for his worn mukluks by the side of the bunk.

"He dreams about Zack. It's one of the reasons I believe Zack is alive. Dogs know a lot. Look! He's using that hind foot!" Kop-a was now fully aroused.

"I'll see to him, Kop-a," said Lucas. "You take it easy. Let him go. I'll follow."

But Kop-a did not seem to hear. He was watching

Moise's right foot as it moved with the rest of his body. "He hasn't done that since he was hurt," he exclaimed. Already Lucas had the door open and all three waited as the crippled dog passed through.

"There's a sled out there," said Lucas, as they hurriedly donned their parkas. "I can hear the bell. But we're off the main trail. I wonder who would be coming this way?"

Moise was using both of his hind feet now, and his fore paws dug frantically into the snow in an effort to hurry. His back bent double and there were short gasping sounds as though he were choking. Suddenly he came to an abrupt halt and a long, piercing howl broke the stillness. Deer, grazing in the valley, raised their heads, startled, and moved to one side as four giant huskies pulling a high-back sled came over the skyline. In the sled's spacious seat was a tiny black dog, and a familiar figure could be seen riding on the runners. A second later, a voice rang out, clear and joyous . . .

"Moise! Good dog, Moise!"

It was Zack Denny!

The meeting which followed was never forgotten. Questions, explanations, laughter and more questions! Zack, alive, safe, weathered by storm and sun, had appeared among them as if dropped from the sky. Lucas, In-a-loo and Kop-a all ran to meet him, Kop-a as unsteady as a newborn fawn but the speediest of all. The big corporal hugged each one in turn as Ruff tore about them in mad circles of joy and Moise lifted his head and gave his wild, weird call which was answered by the dogs in the shed. The deer became excited and two herd boys and the Lapp dog drove them farther down the valley, while Lucas shouted orders at the top of his lungs.

Zack's relief at seeing Kop-a was great, and he seemed deeply appreciative of the boy's efforts to find him. "I was sick with worry until I saw by your tracks that you got mixed up at the ravine and turned east," he said. "Then I knew you'd follow the tundra and reach the coast, providing you escaped the squalls and kept your direction as well as your nerve. It was the longest but the safest way for you to travel. But I never dreamed you'd walk right into Lucas' camp!"

"Where did you come from?" asked Lucas as they all walked toward the igloo, Zack carrying Moise on one shoulder and Ruff panting at Kop-a's heels. "I was just starting out to find you. In-a-loo and I were waiting for Kop-a to wake up when Moise began to act queerly . . ."

"I came down the coast with a sick prisoner. I couldn't follow Kop-a but had to wait until my man could travel. Then we took a short cut across some lakes . . . fell in again, too." He grinned at Kop-a. "We hit the coast west of here and I came as fast as I could to find you, Lucas. I knew Kop-a was coming here first and I thought maybe the two of us together could locate him. You can imagine how glad I was to hear Moise howl and see Kop-a running to meet me!"

"You had a prisoner?" asked Kop-a. "Who was he? Where did you find him? Tell us . . ." They had entered the igloo and In-a-loo hurried to make fresh coffee, listening eagerly as she worked.

"It's quite a story," said Zack, and then as they sat

about the little table he told of his experience in the storm, of his meeting Jean Michaud, otherwise known as Andre Angola in that section, and of the final capture of Mat and Joe Michaud, as well as finding Ruff. The three Michaud brothers, he said, were now under guard in a ranch on the coast about ten miles away.

"They're a peculiar breed," added Zack. "They fight like cats and dogs over little things but they stick together in times of trouble. Jean became very much frightened at the possibility of Joe's dying. His superstitions got the best of him. So he made a full confession and signed it. It was a long, strange tale. But I have a little surprise for you," and he reached into an inner pocket of his doeskin jacket. All three watched in suspense as he brought out a soft roll of pussy willow cotton and laid it before Lucas on the table.

"The labret!" exclaimed Lucas. "I hoped . . . I didn't dare ask . . ."

"Ah-nee-kah!" breathed In-a-loo over his shoulder.

The jadite labret lay before them, a round green button, its delicate carving almost worn smooth by the usage of Lucas' ancestors.

"I shall never be able to thank you," and Lucas' eyes were bright with gratitude. "It may seem strange to you that we of the north value such things so highly. But when I found the stone gone, I felt stripped of my past, my heritage." His fingers caressed the labret as he talked. "My cousins have the mate and we are very proud of them. A trader wanted to buy mine last summer. Andre . . . Jean . . . must have heard about it."

"Leave it to Jean," said Zack. "He has a grapevine

intelligence worthy of the Force. The only reason he pulled me into his igloo out of the storm was because he believed me to be an accomplice. Do you know a boy called Peluk?" All the while Zack's hand was patting Moise's white head which lay across his knee.

"Yes, we know Peluk," exclaimed In-a-loo and Lucas together.

"Peluk was hired by Jean to enter your igloo and steal the bead. Although I searched Jean's things carefully, I could not find it. Can you guess who finally discovered it?"

"No," came from all three listeners.

"Ruff over there," and Zack nodded his head at the small black puppy in Kop-a's lap. "One of Jean's superstitions is squirrels. He traveled with one called Molly. Well, Ruff had his eye on Molly, and the night I left for the Michauds' camp, he chewed his leash in two pieces, upset Molly's box, and chased her outside. The labret was hidden in the bottom of Molly's box. I suppose Ruff was after bits of meat the squirrel had stored away. Anyway, to make a long story short, I came back to find Molly scolding on top of the igloo, Ruff inside asleep with the labret between his paws, and Jean still bound hand and foot and nearly crazy! Ruff had steak that night for supper. He's some pup!"

"And to think it was Andre Angola," said Lucas, as if stunned and unable to believe all he was hearing. "He has not been seen for a long time around here. The last I heard, he was a witch doctor working on the natives up the coast. Some of us complained of his methods and then he disappeared."

"He's going to disappear again for a good long time," replied Zack. "This time it will be jail. His two brothers will go with him, though I think some leniency should be shown Mat, who isn't very bright. Jean has done a lot of damage in many ways, his brothers aiding and abetting him. It was Jean, of course, who mixed the herds, spread the news, and inflamed the herders against you, Lucas. It was his revenge for your interference when he was selling John Buckley's deer on the side. He never forgot."

"Perhaps now," interrupted In-a-loo eagerly, "Mr. Paul will not be so anxious to sell the ranch. If he would only come home . . ."

"Another surprise for you," broke in Zack. "Paul Buckley has come home. He arrived this morning from Ottawa and had hardly taken off his parka when I pulled up at the ranch with the three Michauds and told my story. He seemed pleased for your sake, Lucas, and said he would be over here just as soon as he had opened his mail and tended to a few things."

"Did you say he'd come from Ottawa," asked Lucas, "and not St. Lawrence Island?"

"Yes, he said Ottawa. We locked the Michauds in his back office and I am to go back to the ranch and make it my headquarters until the police plane shows up. Then I'll travel back to Aklavik along the coast and locate some witnesses. Incidentally, I asked Mr. Paul, as you call him, to be on the lookout for a boy if he came along and to tell him I was at Lucas' fawning range. I didn't mention any names," and Zack gave a quick glance at Kop-a.

Silent, tense, Kop-a had been listening to every word, scarcely touching the stew and fresh bread which In-a-loo had placed before him. With a visible effort, as though steeling himself against something which he did not wish to hear, he turned to Zack, his lips scarcely moving, his eyes tortured with hope and doubt.

"Did he say . . . is he selling the ranch?"

"It looks that way," Zack answered gently, after a slight pause. "He had gone to Ottawa to talk with a prospective customer. Look out, Kop-a! Ruff is eating all that nice meat . . ."

But it was too late. Ruff, standing on his hind legs, his forefeet on the table, had licked Kop-a's bowl clean. The boy made no attempt to stop him. He was staring at Lucas.

"The dogs are barking, Lucas," said In-a-loo. She had come close to the table and laid a hand gently on Kop-a's shoulder.

Lucas slowly got to his feet, the misery he had seen in the boy's face reflected in his own.

"Someone's coming," he said.

CHAPTER TWENTY

The Long Trail Ends

FIVE dogs and a sled were almost at the door of the igloo when Lucas led the way outside. A tall, heavy-set man of important bearing in a marmot skin parka brought his team to a stop and hastily stepped from the runners. His darkly tanned face, lined with fatigue and worry, brightened as he caught sight of Zack's sled at the rear of the igloo.

"Lucas!" his deep voice called. "A man named Denny . . . he's here, isn't he? Oh, there you are!" he exclaimed as Zack appeared behind Lucas. "I need help, Corporal. I've just received word from a school in Chicago that my nephew . . ."

Paul Buckley got no further. As if struck speechless, he stood before them, his mouth open, his mittened hand clutching a white crumpled envelope and his dark eyes staring at Kop-a in the doorway.

"John!" He managed to speak at last. "John! WHAT ARE YOU DOING HERE?" His face was flushed a dull red beneath its tan and there was wrathful indignation in the powerful voice.

Kop-a moved forward slowly. Clad in Lucas' parka, which he had put on by mistake in his hurry, he appeared lost in its folds. The bandage on his head drooped over one eye and he pushed it back before he spoke.

"I've come home, Uncle Paul," he answered a trifle unsteadily.

"You've come home? You've come home?" roared Mr. Buckley. "Who said you could come home? Why . . . why, I'm amazed at you! I'm amazed! Here's a letter from Dr. Wing," and he shook the white envelope in the air. "He's had two plain-clothes men hunting for you, and he's half crazy trying to keep things quiet and protect the reputation of the school! Do you mean to say, Corporal," and he now turned angrily on Zack, "that you didn't know who he was . . . you, a Mounted Policeman?"

"No, he didn't know who I was. He didn't know, Uncle Paul," repeated Kop-a earnestly. He had come forward, his timidity gone, and stood by Zack's side. His face was pale beneath the bandage, but he confronted his uncle bravely. "Zack knew I was a friend of Lucas. I told him my name was Kop-a. That's all he knew."

"What he says is true, Mr. Buckley." Zack's voice was easy, affable. He had remembered E. B.'s description of Paul Buckley . . . 'crusty, quick-tempered, but when you once break through the crust, he's all right.'

"I had no idea he was your nephew," Zack continued. "There was no way of identifying him and he didn't confide in me. If he had, I might have felt obliged to report him and he was smart enough to know it. I felt that a boy like him must have some good reason for making such a long hard trip. He's shown courage and grit to get here, and I think it's only fair to hear what he's got to say."

Mr. Buckley stared at them both, his face still perplexed and flushed.

"I had to come, Uncle Paul," and Kop-a took a step nearer. "I sent you a letter but you didn't answer. Then I wrote again and sent Sol's letter, too. Didn't you get them? I waited and waited . . ."

"I didn't receive any letters," answered Mr. Buckley slowly, somewhat mollified. "If they came, they were probably forwarded to Ottawa." He was observing Kop-a carefully now, watching the expression of the boy's face, the way he talked and the way he moved his hands. "What were the letters about?"

"The ranch!" There was a sharp note of agony, of excitement in the young voice. "Did you sell the ranch, Uncle Paul? Did you sell it?"

A dead silence followed, as Kop-a stood motionless in suspense.

"No, I haven't sold the ranch yet." Mr. Buckley's voice was aggravatingly slow. "The papers are made out, but I didn't sign them in Ottawa. I wanted more time to think it over. But why does it mean so much to you, young man? And who's Sol? What's he got to do with it?"

The relief in Kop-a's face was like the sun breaking through clouds. His whole being was alight as he turned to Lucas, a flood of words almost choking him. "The ranch is safe, Lucas! It's safe! He hasn't sold it! I hurried so to get here, Uncle Paul!" he exclaimed, wheeling back toward Mr. Buckley. "Sol is Lucas' cousin! He wrote me about that man. I was afraid the man would buy it . . ."

"What man?"

"Anderson, a man named Anderson. He didn't want it for himself! He was buying for some company and they didn't want you to know it! They're a bunch of chiselers!"

"Corporation," muttered Mr. Buckley. His eyes were alert, his mouth grim.

"Yes, Sol wrote that Anderson would slip it over if he could. I wrote all this and you didn't answer . . ."

"Sol again. How do I know if Sol knows what he's talking about?"

"I know Sol." Zack spoke with quiet assurance, smiling at the surprised inquiry in Kop-a's eyes. "Sol Goodhope is one of the finest guides on the coast. I'd take his word for anything. He used to work here, didn't he?" he asked Lucas.

Lucas nodded silently, his dark eyes on Kop-a. In-a-loo stood close by, anxious and unhappy.

Kop-a went on, almost breathlessly, "Sol heard some men in his party talking. They didn't like Anderson. Said he was a crook and a slick one."

"So Anderson thinks he can slip it over, does he?" Paul Buckley was looking decidedly disturbed. His eyes caught sight of the letter still in his hand and he addressed the boy once more, but there was no anger in his voice. "And you think all this warrants your running away from school and my turning the country upside down to find you?"

"Yes, oh, yes," answered Kop-a, looking up into his uncle's face. "The ranch is home. Father and I lived there together. Father worked hard to make the ranch a success . . . he wouldn't want it sold to the wrong people. All our friends, the Eskimos around here, would suffer. You know they wouldn't get fair prices for their meat and skins."

"I don't wish to sell to the wrong people either, for that matter," agreed Mr. Buckley. "Of course there are corporations and corporations . . . some good and some bad. . . ."

"Uncle Paul, let me stay home!" In his eagerness Kop-a clutched the front of his uncle's parka. He had lost all fear of this big blustering man. "Lucas and I could run the ranch. In-a-loo would take care of us. We planned it three years ago, after Father died. I'm old enough to help now. I'll go to the reindeer school and train. You can carry on your work at the Island and come here when you feel like it . . ."

"That sounds all right," said his uncle, "but what about your education? I sent you to one of the finest schools in the States. You can't grow up into an ignorant . . ."

"I've been there three years," interrupted Kop-a. "It was a swell school and I liked the fellows. But I belong here, Uncle Paul. I could go over to the school at Wellington for part of the year. In the States I had to spend my vacations in other fellows' homes . . . it isn't the same as your own. You and I don't know each other very well, Uncle Paul. But I thought if I could just get here and talk with you . . ." Kop-a's voice choked.

The older man was silent. His expression softened as

he looked down at the tense, eager figure before him, and a flash of pain suddenly crossed his face.

"Lord, boy, but you look like your father," he said quickly, and put a hand on Kop-a's shoulder. "You look like him and you act like him. What's the bandage for?"

"I cut my head on some ice."

"I guess my feet did it," Zack explained. "I had to jump to crash some ice over his head."

"H'm. Guess it's time to clean you up a little. That's one of Lucas' parkas, isn't it? Why on earth are you called Kop-a? Your name is John. John Buckley, Junior. No wonder the Corporal didn't know who you were," his uncle complained testily.

"It means snow-bird," volunteered In-a-loo in her soft voice. The tense atmosphere had been broken and they were all standing close together now. "He was little when his father brought him here . . . without any mother. The kop-a-noos came on his birthday that first spring and I called him 'Kop-a-noo.' After that everyone called him 'Kop-a.' "

"I see." Mr. Buckley seated himself on the edge of his sled, suddenly weary and plainly troubled at the new turn of events. He was touched, in spite of himself, at the sight of his brother's boy. It had been easier for him to send the child away to a good school than to have him around. But had he been right, he wondered?

"Lucas," and Paul Buckley turned now to his top hand. "Lucas, you've been quiet all through this. Would Kop-a be a help to you? You've been overworked. Heaven knows what I'd have done without you! But I don't want to add to your burden. You know our problems . . . the poor shipping facilities, the lack of help. If we can't get our meat on the market, the ranch is a losing proposition. I am under contract on the Island and have my own work to do. I told Anderson to come here next week and we'd talk some more. He seemed very anxious to buy, but to tell the truth, I never liked the man and I held off. If he represents some crooked gang I'll kick him from here to Halifax!" Mr. Buckley's face began to grow red again. "What do you say, Lucas? I don't know much about boys. I only saw Kop-a once and that was three years ago. Could you two manage together?"

"Yes, yes, Mr. Paul." Lucas was eager, his dark eyes shining. "Kop-a would be a great help. It is what we both wish. I'll do anything rather than have the ranch sold. It is our home, too," and he patted In-a-loo's hand on his sleeve. "Mr. John was awfully good to us. We loved the ground he walked on and we love his son. In time, he will take his father's place. I don't know what to say about the shipping, sir."

"I think I know why Anderson is so anxious to buy." Zack stroked Moise's head as he talked. "You know, the Force gets news ahead of other people sometimes. Before I left Aklavik, I heard them talking at the post about the new line of shipping boats coming through here. Undoubtedly Anderson and the company he represents know all about it. And if I'm not mistaken, Anderson is the same man who bought ahead for some company on the Alaskan coast. He offered high prices to the natives for their herds and they sold out. They didn't know what to do with so much money and it raised the devil with them. I think your shipping problem will work out all right, Mr. Buckley. Within the year."

"Well, that's good news," and Paul Buckley drew in a deep breath. "You and my nephew seem to have managed pretty well together." For the first time he smiled at them both. "I haven't told you, Corporal Denny, how much I appreciate your good work in capturing your three prisoners. I hope it means a new stripe on your sleeve."

"Thank you, sir."

"He's already won the gold crossed-rifle badge, Uncle Paul. He's one of the best shots on the Force!" Kop-a's admiration of Zack was more than a little apparent.

"I don't doubt it," replied his uncle.

"There are many fine shots on the Force," said Zack modestly. "By the way, Kop-a," and the young corporal turned to the boy, anxious to change the subject, "I've been noticing a paw hanging from my sled. What have you got under the tarpaulin? Have you been hunting? is that why Moise is lame? You didn't have any gun . . ." Without waiting for an answer, he walked over to the sled, followed by Lucas and Moise.

"Moise tackled a grizzly. I haven't had time to tell you about it. He was alone and I had to let the other dogs out to help him. They had an awful fight. I used the ice chisel," explained Kop-a.

"The ice chisel!" Zack stopped and looked at him, somewhat aghast. Then he and Lucas removed the canvas and rolled the big brown skin out on the snow, the trap beside it. Moise growled, showing he had not forgotten.

"My word!" exclaimed Zack. "He's a nice one. Well, Kop-a, you got your bear! And with an ice chisel!" He held up the chisel for Mr. Buckley to see. The long wooden handle was still stained with the bear's blood.

"Yes, he had that trap on one foot." The boy was happy, excited.

"Let me see that trap," said Mr. Buckley to Lucas who was examining it.

"Yes, sir. It's one of ours, sir," observed Lucas, giving it to him.

"I thought so. One of our new traps." Mr. Buckley did not seem to have much to say but stared silently at his nephew, the trap dangling from his mittened hand.

"I didn't finish skinning him," said Kop-a. "I thought you'd help me out later, Lucas. He was pretty heavy to handle. I've always wanted to hang a skin of my own beside that one of Father's at the ranch. This one isn't as large as Father's, though."

"It's large enough," commented Mr. Buckley gruffly. "If those claws had ripped into you once, you'd have known it. Lucas, I think that was the bear that was troubling the herds this spring. We bought heavier traps to hold him but I see they didn't do the work. Well, you seem able to take care of yourself, my boy. Hard trip, was it?" Mr. Buckley had risen to his feet.

"Yes, sir. I thought I'd never get here. And you *are* going to let me stay, aren't you, Uncle Paul?" The dark eyes were pleading, the voice eager and hopeful.

Mixed emotions were evident in Mr. Buckley's face.

Worry, joy and sorrow were there, and he seemed to be sparring for time as he drew a long breath. "We'll see, we'll see. Let's go inside where it's warm. I didn't have much for breakfast. Have you any coffee left, In-a-loo? And Kop-a, you'd better get cleaned up a bit and we'll go home and wire Dr. Wing you're safe. That letter took about ten years out of me. I'm afraid, Kop-a, that you've got a cranky old fuddy-duddy for an uncle. But we'll get on . . . we'll get on."

Mr. Buckley's arm was around his young nephew's shoulders as they entered the igloo together, and bits of conversation floated back to Zack and Lucas who were following.

"Lord, boy, but you do look like your father. I never realized . . . I guess you've earned the right to stay . . . It will be nice having you down here in the north with us . . . Your father would have loved to have seen that bearskin . . . Does the little black dog belong to you?"

It was hard to say good-bye that last morning at the Buckley ranch. The dogs were harnessed and ready to go, and Kop-a moved among them, patting and calling each one by name. Susie whimpered, Barry bit at the top of his fur boot as if to keep him near, and the rest of the dogs wagged their tails with the air of old, established friends. At last he came to Moise who had insisted on taking his place as lead dog. In spite of Moise's lameness, Zack had decided to let him run a little way. The big white dog stood motionless as Kop-a drew near.

"Good-bye, Moise." Once more he put out his hand

a little uncertainly, remembering the approach he had made to the lead dog the first night of their escape from the Michauds. Since then, much had happened and they had spent many hours together. Had he made any gain in the dog's affections?

Kop-a's face must have shown his anxiety and concern, for Zack, standing near, spoke.

"Don't be disappointed if he doesn't notice you . . ." Then he stopped suddenly. For Moise had taken a step forward. Ever so lightly, ever so briefly, the dog touched the outstretched hand with his black nose and then stepped into his place again. The simple dignified gesture stirred the hearts of all watching.

Good-byes had been said several times, Mr. Buckley thanking Zack for his kindness to Kop-a, Lucas silently shaking hands with a world of gratitude shining in his face, and Kop-a hovering near, unable to find the words which would express his feelings. Then came the crack of the whip and the sled moved. But instead of spurting ahead as usual, the dogs started out slowly, several of them looking back to see if Kop-a were coming. Automatically the boy followed, running beside Zack at an even pace.

"You'll be coming back?"

"May come through any day."

"Do you think you'll be made a sergeant?"

"Not sure. I'll let you know."

"Uncle Paul and Lucas say Ruff has Lapp blood. He can be trained to guard the herds."

"Fine. He'll make a good herd dog."

And still the feet kept alongside the sled. They had now reached a level space with the bend of the coast line ahead.

"Tell Mrs. Henry to come down. She can paint her picture here."

"I'll do that," Zack promised.

"Moise seems to be running all right."

"Stepping right along. He's your friend now."

"I'll leave you . . . pretty soon, I guess." Kop-a's breathing was becoming labored as the dogs began to pick up speed.

"Good-bye, Kop-a!"

"Good-bye, Zack!"

The feet stopped and the sled went on. There was a final wave as the dogs raced ahead. And in the clear cold morning air, the bell could be heard long after the sled had turned the bend.

CAPE BATHURST
CAPE
BEAUFORT SEA
FAWNING GROUNDS
ANDERSON RIVER
LOST LANDS
AKLAVIK
IVORY HORN LAKE
GRAPEVINE FORKS
KOPA'S TRAIL FROM U.S.A.
MACKENZIE RIVER
GOOD HOPE
YUKON
J. C. WONSETLER